STELLA'S CARPET

STELLA'S CARPET

A Novel

LUCY E.M. BLACK

| N₁ | O₂ | N₁ |
CANADA

*Publisher's note: This book is a work of fiction. Names, characters, places and
incidents are either the product of the author's imagination or are used
fictitiously, and any resemblance to actual persons living or dead
is entirely coincidental.*

Library and Archives Canada Cataloguing in Publication

Title: Stella's carpet : a novel / Lucy E.M. Black.

Names: Black, Lucy E. M., 1957– author

Identifiers: Canadiana 20210257229 | ISBN 9781989689264 (softcover)

Classification: LCC PS8603.L2555 S74 2021 | DDC C813/.6—dc23

Printed and bound in Canada on 100% recycled paper.

Now Or Never Publishing
901, 163 Street
Surrey, British Columbia
Canada V4A 9T8

nonpublishing.com
Fighting Words.

We gratefully acknowledge the support of the Canada Council for the Arts
and the British Columbia Arts Council for our publishing program.

In Loving Memory
Mum en Tante Co

A Persian rug is perfectly imperfect and precisely imprecise.
~ Persian Proverb

Give sorrow words; the grief that does not speak whispers
the o'er-fraught heart and bids it break.
~ Macbeth

The rose and the thorn, and sorrow and gladness are linked together.
~ Saadi

The weaving of textiles, whether tapestries, cloth, or carpets, has been documented since before 2000 BCE. Weaving involves the use of two threads that are interlaced vertically and horizontally. This can be done on a hand loom, a backstrap loom, or an automated mechanical device. The looms can be primitive, portable units used by nomadic peoples or they can be factory-based machines ranging from the very small to the large. The threads can be cotton, wool, hemp, silk, or a blending of contemporary fibres, and these threads must be spun and dyed. Dyes such as the beloved blue indigo and warm yellow saffron are often processed from plants. Mineral-based dyes, such as the bright green that comes from malachite, or insect-based dyes like the rich Tyrian purple made by boiling snails, or contemporary synthetic dyes can all be used. The patterns can be modern in design or follow traditional markings, with shapes and motifs that have been passed down through many generations of weavers. Traditional carpets that replicate older patterns and colours tell us stories that only an experienced eye can discern. Carpets of Delight *is about those stories. We want you to understand the history and significance woven into these carpets. We wish for you to appreciate carpets not merely as useful in decorating your homes but as objects that delight you with their colours, design, symbolism, and provenance.*

Stella had practised reading the Introduction a dozen times. She needed to sound confident and knowledgeable while making the book sound interesting. Her father, along with Parisa and Parvez, had chosen her to read at the book launch. They'd be there to cheer her on and answer questions, but she'd be the one at the microphone. Stella knew they'd have difficulty reading from Fatima's book without breaking down. This was something she could do for them.

She stepped into her black dress and smoothed her unruly dark hair into a tight knot that sat low on the nape of her neck. Her mother might critique the attempt later, but she was doing her best to achieve an understated elegance for the event. Next came dark eyeliner, black pointed pumps, a spray of perfume. The overall effect pleased her: surprisingly classic and polished. Stella was tall and thin and tended to slouch self-consciously. Tonight she wanted to stand upright and look sophisticated.

Pam and Tony were going out for dinner first and meeting her there. Stella would be driving down by herself and needed to allow time for delays on the Parkway. She rushed out to her car and began the long commute to the Whisky Walk—a complex of Victorian buildings that formed a once substantial whisky plant on the edge of the lake. The place had been recently reimagined as a tourist area and was now filled with restaurants, boutiques, and art galleries. The launch would be held in one of its larger galleries, one that had housed the big copper vats where the whisky was distilled. The gallery owner had removed the vats but left in place a spiderweb of fat copper piping and industrial pieces that together gave off a warm patina. She'd spent the morning there, helping to put up carpets where contemporary paintings normally hung.

As she drove, Stella contemplated all that had happened leading up to this night. How to summarize a brother, two adopted cousin-friends and co-authors, the loss of her grandfather, the death of Fatima, and the ridiculous man who seemed to dote on her mother? It had been an emotional time, and yet, she realized now, she'd never felt more content.

THE BOOK LAUNCH

The crowd was well-dressed. Most seemed to know one another and sipped at their white wine in small, intimate groups. Stella inserted herself into the throng, spying designer purses, high-end fashion, flashes of expensive jewellery. Still, she felt on display as she navigated the room, looking for William. People were nodding at her, taking notice of her movements. Evidently she'd been identified, and that made her nervous.

Her father reached for her arm and led her gently to the bar, where a reading light and a microphone had been carefully positioned. She hadn't been daunted by these earlier in the day, with the warm sunlight flooding the room, but now, in the black of the evening and amid the din of animated chatter, Stella began to second-guess her willingness to read. Moving towards the microphone, she faltered, her hand poised above the slender device.

It was Tony who spoke to her—*Make us proud, kid*—and his remark, so unexpected, gave her the stamina to pick up the microphone, flick on the button, and begin.

Good evening. I would like to ask you to join me. In just a moment I'd like to begin reading to you from an important new book, Carpets of Delight. *It was written by my stepmother, Fatima Surin-Wheeler, and was a work of great love.*

EDELWEISS

Two tarnished silver brooches lay in a basket of discarded jewellery. They didn't look valuable, but they were unusual. Stella picked them up and turned them over. There was no pin to fasten them with; instead, they had tiny holes where you could stitch them into place. The flowered centres were gold and stood out against the blackened silver. Stella recognized the flower as edelweiss. If she polished them, she thought they might look pretty sewn onto a jacket lapel. She placed them on the counter's scratched glass surface.

The sound prompted the proprietor to look up from his reading. He stood slowly, arching his back, and made his way towards her, shuffling as though he were afraid of lifting his feet from the dusty floor. Did he suspect, she wondered, that he'd float upward if he raised a foot? Was this grounded shuffle an attempt to stay anchored?

Them's old, he said, breaking the silence. *Five dollars, if you're ready.*

Thank you. She laid a crisp unfolded bill on the counter.

He reached down and picked up an old piece of newspaper from the floor. Placing it on the glass, opaque with the residue of many hands, he put the brooches on one corner of the newsprint and rolled them expertly, taping the paper tightly and with a flourish. Stella smiled stiffly, took the little package, and put it in her bag.

You have a good day now, he called as she made her way out the door.

The shop had been crowded with merchandise and dimly lit with a haze of yellow light. She'd lost herself in the strangeness of it all. Once beloved items were stacked haphazardly on rough wooden shelves or left piled in open boxes on the floor. Strangers pawing through the artifacts of a life. The smell of damp basements and garages permeated the shop, a whiff of death.

Why would anyone want to buy someone else's junk? thrummed in her head. It was her mother's voice, displeased and critical.

THE HOUSE

*W*e've got enough of our own junk, she complained when Stella returned to the house. *Don't be bringing more home. It could be full of bugs and germs. People die from those things now. That Ebola virus melts your insides out. Is that what you want to happen?*

The shrillness was unpleasant to Stella. The voice kept her from unwrapping her treasure and showing the brooches to her mother. *Look!* she wanted to say. *Just look!* Instead Stella moved to the kitchen, silently filled the kettle, and settled into the domestic routine of placating. She walked softly on the sage-green broadloom. It was a soundless house in waiting.

Stella was accustomed to the serenity of the house and found some comfort in the familiar. There was a harmony in their lives that grounded her, that allowed her to venture out in short forays to work and to grocery shop and to run mundane errands.

THE FATHER

You will always be my little star, her father had assured her before he left. *I will always love you and I will always love your mother. I need to do this for us all.*

Her mother claimed not to know why he left. In his last Christmas card, the photograph showed him confident and smiling. A Tabriz carpet, its tendrils reaching from the central medallion, curled and snaked around his feet. All three people in the photo were beautiful. The woman: her hair sleek and well styled, lips outlined in deep red, a simple black dress, a nose that was perhaps a bit wide, but lovely teeth and a friendly smile. The child: a shock of long dark hair, red flushed cheeks, a smiling little mouth. The man: a dark grey suit with white shirt and a green striped tie, hair greying slightly in places, one hand on his new wife's leg and the other encircling his son. The smiles were satisfied and easy. Stella had the photo slipped inside the frame of her bathroom mirror. She looked at it each morning when she washed her face and brushed her teeth.

Hello Dad, she would sometimes say. *How are you today?* She didn't know the name of the woman or the boy or she'd greet them too, willing them to become a part of her life, her almost family. They would welcome her into their lives and into their house with its brick fireplace and Persian carpets that were lived on. She'd never been invited to that house. She'd never been

introduced to these strangers who had appropriated her father
and displaced her mother.

THE STAR CARPET

At first, her father would call her every week at her dorm.
How's my Star? was how he'd begin each time. A forced
intimacy. Gradually the frequency declined.

He'd driven her to Victoria College, helped her move into
residence, stood for hours in line with her at the bookstore to pay
for her books. He'd lugged a mini-fridge and toaster oven up the
wooden staircase and then surprised her with a real gift: a small
Persian carpet that he unrolled beside her narrow bed.

The rug was a geometric patterned piece in wool. *Sixty-four
knots per inch*, her father informed her. The central image was a
Lesghi Star. *I knew this one was for you the minute I saw it. Stars are
rare, you know. They weave them only in the mountains, near eastern
Turkey. This one is nineteenth century. From Dagestan. Very good
spacing.* Her father stroked the carpet while he spoke, straighten-
ing it and patting it down on top of the soiled grey Berber in her
dorm. It imposed an unexpected island of colour and richness in
the shabby room. *It's a good investment. It'll be worth a lot more
someday. I knew you'd love it.* Stella noted his satisfaction and felt
warmed by it. She understood that the carpet was a deeply personal offering.

He reminded her that green was the holy colour of the
Prophet, signifying hope, renewal, and life, and that red was the
colour of beauty, wealth, courage, luck, joy, and truth. The
colours in her carpet were a blessing, and a wish. Hands far away
and before she was born had woven this destiny for her. Her
father had chosen carefully.

She loved the carpet. On her first night in the dorm room
she slept on her stomach so that she could stroke it with a dan-
gling hand before drifting off to sleep. Over the years, she too
had been seduced by the beauty of her father's collection. She'd
loved patting the nap while they hung cool and still from the

ceiling-mounted racks in their specially designed basement vault. The flowered carpets from Kerman were among her favourites. The subdued colours of the rugs from Nain moved her too. She had learned to recognize such things as the warp fringes at the ends, weft threads made of silk, carpets with five hundred knots per square inch. Throughout her adolescence she had followed her father's growing obsession. She quickly absorbed enough vocabulary and knowledge to enter into his hobby. Years later she would question her motives and wonder if she was just trying to keep him from slipping away entirely.

Stella had been as surprised as her mother when he announced he'd developed *other interests*. He'd met the woman who was to become his second wife at a rug convention. She worked for one of the importing houses he dealt with and had published articles on the social significance of Persian carpets and their provenance. Stella had cyber-stalked her for a while in an attempt to understand how this woman could lure her quiet, reserved father away from the carpets in their basement, out of his routines and commitments, and into another life. Stella wanted to possess that kind of power. To draw him back.

The Lesghi Star rug remained in Stella's dorm room until she graduated, but long before then she'd rolled it up and tucked it under her bed, hidden from view. Sarah, a friend from Intro to Ancient Civ, had made a big fuss about the carpet when she first saw it. *Is that for real?* she'd asked. *A real Persian carpet? Do you know how those things are made? They use child labour and they totally exploit women and children.*

My father gave it to me. He collects them.

That's awful. I can't believe it! What are you going to do?

Do?

Well, you can't keep it, it's an outrage.

It was a gift. It has my name woven in the pattern.

Still, said Sarah, *nobody should see it. It's awful to have.*

Stella had been shaken by this. It had never occurred to her that the women and children who made such beautiful things might be taken advantage of. As a teenager, she'd been taught to value the workmanship and the history of these pieces, to appreciate the regional differences, the knotting techniques, the degree of depression in the warp thread. She'd thought of them only as beautiful objects. And so, ashamed, she rolled the rug into a tight cylinder and kept it hidden.

TEACHING

The Persian rug was now in her bedroom at home, a little less brilliant than it had once been but still lovely. Her rooms and the kitchen were alone in having escaped her mother's broadloom. The feel of the cool, polished pine floor against her bare feet was satisfying. She'd stand on carpet in the winter when the floor was cold, tracing her toes along the patterned border as she dressed.

She had a little car, but the school was close to home and she preferred to walk. Besides which, she always felt self-conscious driving it. It was far too flashy for her, she felt. It had been a graduation present from her father. He'd asked the dealership to wrap it. *For twenty-five thousand dollars, the least they can do is gift-wrap.* He'd been pleased with his joke and delighted by her surprise. The bow must have been four feet across and was fastened to the front hood. The salesman removed it with a flourish when Stella drove off the lot. Her foot tapped the brake and she hesitated. It seemed ungrateful to stop the car and demand the bow back. Her father would be embarrassed. But the taking of the bow irked her.

Stella packed her marking, her day book, and her lunch into a big nylon backpack. The painted letters had creased and become worn over time. It now read *University -f Toronto* across the flap. The little "o" had worn off; it was in the centre of the flap and had received the most contact. *F Toronto* amused her. She felt smug walking to school and back each day with its secret message. *F Toronto*, she thought. *F the stupid staff meeting.* Neither of these things could she say aloud.

She'd felt nervous when she stood in front of the class for the first time and called out their names. She worried they wouldn't like her, that she'd be discovered as a fraud and be driven from the building. Her B.A. and B.Ed. should have equipped her for this, should have given her the confidence she needed to face down the boys with their blackheads and oversized jeans. She was, after all, *the cream of the crop*. As they'd been told in the panelled auditorium on their first day of teachers' college. *Only the very best, the very brightest, the most qualified students were given admittance to this prestigious program*. She'd graduated *magna cum laude*. She was as well educated as anyone. She'd wanted to continue her studies: a master's and then a Ph.D. in Victorian studies.

What good would that do you? her mother had snapped. *A teaching degree is all you need. Job security and benefits. Be a teacher. Leave all the fancy jobs to someone else.*

Her father had offered to fund graduate school, but Stella had declined. She'd never crossed the border or even travelled outside the province; she'd never flown or taken a train. It wasn't death and carnage she feared so much as being exposed and vulnerable, not knowing how to navigate. How could she conduct research without visiting the British Library and the Victoria & Albert? How could she fully comprehend the world she read about without experiencing, firsthand, the flavour of it? And so her mother provided the rope that moored her and hid her fears. Stella had confessed this to no one.

Waldham was the town where Stella lived. One hour and fifteen minutes from Toronto. She taught at Waldham Collegiate and Vocational Institute, established in 1928 and expanded in stages over the years. Stella loved the school. She loved that you could walk through the postmodern glass entrance and three minutes later be standing in a heritage building with hardwood floors, wainscotting, and eighteen-foot ceilings with Palladian windows. She loved the burnished wooden railings, the oak lecterns for teaching, the ridiculous little offices and washrooms with half-steps up and down in utterly inexplicable places. She loved the stinky sock smell of the gym with its full-length viewing gallery and the echoes of cheering and clapping that seemed to emanate from its walls. She loved the old plaques and trophies that filled the front hallway showcases, and the library with its carefully archived collection of photographs and yearbooks.

Stella had herself graduated from Waldham. Crossed and recrossed the stage self-consciously, having collected a large share of the awards for academic distinction. Her name was inscribed on the Honour Roll, the Governor General's Medal, the Waldham Mayor's Trophy, the Seaman's Memorial Plaque, and the Legion's Award for Patriotism. She averted her eyes when she walked past these. Her life as a student was then, and this life was now.

Occasionally, one of her own students would ask if it was *her* name on an award, and she would reluctantly acknowledge that she'd once been a student in this very classroom. It had been a more difficult adjustment than one would expect. A few of her former teachers were still on staff, and she could not make herself call them by their given names. Mrs. Wooten, for instance, the history teacher, suited *Mrs. Wooten* in a way that *Lynda* did not. *Lynda* lacked the elegance and formality that Mrs. Wooten deserved. And Mr. Vaughan, the math and physics teacher, a scrawny, underfed-looking man, did not at all suit *Ben*. *Mr. Vaughan* afforded him some much-needed dignity.

Stepping behind her desk, Stella began to collect her binders and folders and organize herself for second period. Her students piled out the door, some of them smiling and half waving at her as they left. It wasn't cool to be too friendly with a teacher, she knew, and these small gestures mattered to her. She would hoard them silently as the day progressed, and measure herself by the small count. Thank-you notes, little half waves—these were the treasures she kept close to her heart.

MOORED

When her mother had developed arthritis, Stella moved home to help with the house. The condition reduced Pam's mobility, strength, and willingness to function independently. Stella gradually became housebound, leaving only for school, to shop, or to take her mother to appointments. Her father delicately suggested that this was a mistake. Stella, feeling uncharacteristically defensive, found herself arguing.

William expressed his views mildly and quietly, but Stella, who'd buried her anger at having been left alone to deal with her mother, came out fighting. She accused him of contributing to the slavery and abuse of seven-year-old boys who were taken from their family homes and forced to make rugs in village factories where they developed lung disease and permanently damaged their eyesight.

Her father recoiled at her words. He was stricken. *I only buy rugs from reputable dealers. My wife knows which factories pay decent wages to their workers, and the contemporary ones are Rugmarked to confirm that no child labour was used.* He was getting red in the face now. *Besides which, most of my rugs are antique pieces, which you very well know. I will not be held responsible for the practices of factory masters two hundred years ago.*

Stella had never seen her father so upset. Not even when he'd invited her and her mother to the vault to break the news about his *other interests;* not when Pam had pulled a Shiraz from the overhead rack, ripping at the fringe with her fingers and awkwardly flinging at him what strands she could tear loose in her rage; not when Stella had silently reached for the carpet and pressed it against her body, patting the silk threads in a comforting gesture. She was glad to have aroused such feelings in him.

WILLIAM AND PAMELA

Her mother was irritable when Stella went downstairs. The pain in her joints had been particularly bad this day. She was hungry. She hadn't enjoyed *that quiche thing* for lunch.

It's better hot, Mom, said Stella. *I told you that this morning.*

I won't use that microwave; those rays kill people.

You know that's not true. It was only the first generation that were a problem.

Well, I don't believe you! They just covered it up so we'd buy them. If you stand too close, it'll make you sterile.

Oh, Mom, you worry.

Of course I worry. What else do I have to do? You just go ahead and believe everything you're told.

Stella felt herself stiffening—a familiar response to the tension of living carefully with someone in a precarious emotional and physical state. She began making their dinner with meticulous care, concentrating on each individual task. If she did things perfectly, if she prepared a pleasing meal, then maybe she could escape once again to her room, to her computer and the internet. Her marking could wait, and a few hours alone would make a difference.

They ate quietly on TV tables in the living room: pork chops and apple sauce, fried potatoes and onions, asparagus spears. Her mother ate quickly, shoving forkfuls into her mouth before she'd finished chewing. Stella tried not to watch. It had happened when Pamela had been much alone. If Stella had eaten that way as a child her father would have sent her from the table.

Sometimes Stella closed her eyes and willed herself to remember when such things had begun to slip. Was it before her father left or was it after? Was this why William had developed his *other interests*, or were those *other interests* why her mother had relinquished so many layers of civility?

Stella's parents had met in High Park when her father was studying dentistry. He rented the third-floor flat of Pam's parents' house on Indian Grove. William ate most of his meals at the university and studied at the library. He was rarely home.

Pamela's parents were displaced Poles who had emigrated after the war. Maria didn't think she'd ever have children, having starved for so long during the war that her courses never came with regularity. They were proud of their *real Canadian daughter* and worked hard to ensure she had opportunities. At sixteen, Pam began working at a local restaurant. It happened to be where William habitually ate his Sunday evening meal—he'd bring along his thick dentistry books, spread these out on the checkered tablecloth, and study there until closing. He awkwardly began to tip her when she served him. Then he'd walk her home at the end of her shift.

Their conversations were stilted at first. He was a university student, and her parents had instilled in her the importance of what they called *the intelligentsia* in a new country like Canada. *You could go to university too, you know*, William had once said to her.

I would like that, maybe, someday.

And William allowed himself to become attracted to her. He tried to believe that this beautiful adolescent girl, shy and obliging, would grow into his helpmate and partner. They would marry and he would support her while she went to university and they would build a life together. This is what William told Stella. This was how he fell in love with her mother. *But she never wanted to go. Even when we could afford it, she just didn't want to go. Not even one course.*

Stella had seen photographs taken of them during this time. Her trim mother in tight black pedal pushers and a crisp cotton blouse tucked in smartly. The buttons undone just a little daringly. Her dark, shoulder-length hair combed and straight and held in place with a wide hairband. She stared at the camera defiantly, a half smile on her lips, as if holding in a secret. One hand on her hip, the other holding William's hand. And the look of sheer pleasure her father had as he gazed down at Pamela. *Look at what I have*, it shouted, *look at what I've found*. Stella imagined she could see the chemistry between them, all these years later, captured in that one look of her father's.

When Stella had asked her mother about the same story, she heard a different version. *He wanted me from the first day*, Pam began. *Like a hungry dog, he followed me everywhere. I never had a minute's peace from the day he moved in. I didn't have a choice.*

Mom! You can't mean that. Didn't you love him?

He was always there watching me, his hands everywhere. In the end, there was no choice. It was decided.

Didn't you love him at all?

Love him? Who knows what love is when you're young? He was handsome and clean and had a profession. I knew he would be a good provider. I went to his room and he begged me to marry him. He was full of big ideas and such plans. We married. Maybe love came after.

You were married for nineteen years. Are you telling me you're not sure you loved him?

Stella, listen. How can I be sure? He left me. That is not love.

THE FIRST CARPET

It was hard to say when his interest in carpets really began. He'd grown up in a big house with British Axminster carpets but hadn't really appreciated them. They were part of the landscape of his family home—a small detail in the changes wrought by his mother's decorators. His own room, for instance, had been completely "redone" while he was at camp one summer. He came home to discover that his collection of dog-eared comic books had been disposed of. His bedroom had been painted in a muted olive green colour, with striped brown drapes and matching bedspread. William hated stripes. He hated that people he didn't know had been in his personal space. He wondered if he was the final piece the decorators had selected for the room. Had the room itself been given precedence over him?

In a conscious act of rebellion, he accidentally burned a cigarette hole in the bedspread. He inadvertently pulled the drapes too hard and ripped a panel. He left dirty socks and underwear strewn on the floor and under the bed. He dumped things on the wooden desk and scratched the lacquered finish. But no matter how subversive he was, the room healed itself. A replica bedspread appeared. The drapery panel was sent out for repair. A large blotter appeared on the desk. Socks and underwear disappeared into the laundry. There was no admonishment. There was simply the inevitable return to the spare military order of a green and brown striped room.

Having finished his undergraduate degree, William was accepted into the University of Toronto's dental school. Moving out of the green and brown stripes and into rented rooms was a liberating experience. At the end of the summer, he simply filled his car with clothes and books and moved in. Everything he needed by way of bedding and personal necessities he bought at

Honest Ed's. It wasn't so much that he needed to watch his budget as that he loved the congestion and disorder real people created in the labyrinth of discount offerings. The daily specials delighted him. *Four toothbrushes for a dollar. Ten rolls of toilet paper for a dollar. Shampoo in giant jugs for two dollars. Fresh chickens for two dollars and fifty cents.* And it didn't seem to matter what the special was, William noticed; everyone gravitated to the deal of the day. And so he, like the crowds of other shoppers, studied the featured specials before moving on in search of the items on his list.

His landlords, the Lipinskis, had a worn Persian carpet in their living room. The fibres had been trodden down and there were patches where the grid of underlying threads was exposed, but the richness of the colours still prevailed. Despite its age and condition, the rug filled the room with a vibrant energy. Wine and sapphire and mustard were intricately woven in combinations of diamonds and medallions with yellow birds floating in the sea of colour. Its otherness intrigued him; it spoke to him of worlds he did not know.

On a whim, when walking near the St. Lawrence Market one Saturday morning, he stopped to admire a little carpet artfully displayed in an open-air stand. *You like?* asked the vendor. *Very cheap, I can give you.*

How cheap?

Hundred dollars.

Fifty, countered William.

No, ninety-five dollars and I give you a deal.

Eighty, said William.

No, I no do eighty dollars. Very good quality. Made in Kurdistan. Very old. Many tiny knots. Two years to making.

William reached into his back pocket and pulled out his wallet. Ninety dollars bought the carpet. It wasn't very large. Not much bigger than a bathmat, really. But the colours were seductive and the pattern strangely soothing: saw-edged diamonds fitted together in random order, each filled with a C-shaped design in a contrasting colour. William rolled the rug tightly and placed it under his arm. At home, alone in his little room, he would unroll this treasure on his bed and stroke the fibres with his hands while he examined it carefully.

He had many questions about the carpet—questions that would return to him when he was working on his courses. They niggled at him when he was bored and gave him a sense of purpose when he was at the library. *First, finish this assignment and then spend one hour doing carpet research.* That was William's strategy. In the disciplined way in which he'd been taught to approach life, he began his study of the carpets.

THE SECOND CARPET

He bought his second rug after his first dental extraction. The patient was a girl in her late teens. By the time William and his fellow students had X-rayed and studied every angle of her mouth, the girl had begun to tremble. Under the watchful eye of his mentor, he successfully froze the area and checked his tools. He was aware that his armpits had begun to perspire and worried that the smell conveyed his fear. He was angry that his own body had betrayed him and felt sure it would lead to a colossal failure. In the end, the tooth was extracted in several pieces and he left the girl with what would develop into a deep bruise on her upper chest where he'd accidentally pressed his elbow down in an effort to get leverage. His mentor and a dental assistant finished the job while William escaped with his dignity and pride only slightly diminished.

Walking aimlessly through the streets, he stopped abruptly in front of a dirty glass storefront. A flimsy neon sign announced *Sale Today.* Inside the window were three or four chairs with carpets draped across them. Tidy piles of carpets were laid out on the floor of the shop in rectangular islands of colour, their height varying from a few inches to several feet. A couple of older gentlemen sat on one of the higher piles eating what appeared to be a picnic. William watched for a moment and then stepped inside. A string with brass bells jangled when he opened the door. The men stopped eating and turned to look at him.

Welcome, said the older of the two. *Please. Come in. Have a look around. We have many beautiful carpets to see.*

Thank you, said William. *I'm not really serious about buying one, I just wanted to look. If that's okay.*

No problem, smiled the same man, *no problem at all. Look. Touch. See how beautiful they are.* And with that he turned his back on William and began talking with his friend in soft, sonorous tones.

William approached the chairs first. The carpets were small and stiff. The fibres rough. These were only an imitation of beauty. Even to his inexpert eye, there was something unpleasant and cheap about the sampling. Disappointed, he moved to the first of the rectangular piles. This was more like it. The thread was fine and soft to the touch. The fringe was a lovely border of complex knots and tassels, all of it smooth and seductive to the touch. The colours were opulent—ivories and golds and blues and reds and browns—but so subdued that the overall effect was a subtle blending of richness. An intricate border of yellow flowers outlined the carpet. In the centre was a large medallion with a profusion of adjoining flowers and leaves and two smaller, differently coloured medallions to balance the middle one.

He examined the pattern carefully, looking for repeats, trying to imagine how many people had helped to weave it and how long it had taken. He didn't notice that the men had left off eating and were now standing near him, watching. *You like this one?* asked the younger man. *You have good taste. This is a copy of a Herati carpet, made in Herat, which was in Persian Empire, three hundred years ago. It is not a typical design. It is very special.*

I had no idea they could all be so different.

Yes, come, I show you. Moving to a larger pile of carpets, the salesman began flipping up the corners until he found the one he was looking for. *Look, the Tree of Life. The pattern is the same on the back as on the front. This is a good carpet. It means many small knots and good workmanship.*

William drew near. *It's shiny*, he said. *It doesn't look like the others.*

It is silk, replied the older salesman. *Fine Persian carpets are made in silk also. You tell where a carpet was made by materials and colour and pattern. This one was made in Morocco. Come. Touch. It won't hurt.*

William stroked the carpet tentatively. It was sleek under his hands and surprisingly cool to the touch. *I can't afford these, I'm just a student.*

Ah, said the younger man, *we have carpets for all prices. And today we have a sale. Tell me which one you like and I tell you if we can make something happen. Take your time. Look at everything.*

Thank you.

The men returned to their picnic and seemed engaged in using a small portable stove to make tea. William approached a pile of carpets and flipped up the corners just as he'd seen the men do. Then he peered carefully at the colours and the detail on each one. He knew that he didn't know enough about what he was seeing to fully appreciate the carpets, but he also knew that they were beautiful and somehow full of promise. Resolved, he approached the salesmen. *What do these start at, if you don't mind me asking?*

Anything is possible, smiled the older man. *We have all prices.*

That one over there. William pointed to the carpet with the yellow flowered border. *The copy from Herat.*

Ah, I knew you liked. On sale today.

William wanted a number. He wanted it to be out of reach. But he also wanted the carpet. The salesmen knew it, and William knew they knew it. The three of them stood together looking at the carpet, each unwilling to begin the negotiation. It seemed disrespectful somehow, unseemly—as though they were standing in an art gallery trying to put a price tag on a Renoir.

In the end, he bought the Herati carpet. It wasn't priced. There was no price list. The value of the carpet was a secret kept by the "carpet masters" acting as salesmen. They would reveal the value only when they were sure their buyer was worthy. Then began the negotiations. William didn't know that this process was also part of the exchange. When he left the shop, however, he felt satisfied. He did wonder briefly whether he'd been given the sale price, but the excitement of owning a second carpet, on top of the intoxication of having pulled his first tooth, filled him with a deep sense of happiness.

Opening the front door, he saw that Mr. Lipinski had come in just before him and was still removing his shoes.

William, greeted the old man, *how are you this day? What is that you are carrying?*

A carpet, smiled William. *I bought myself a carpet.*

It looks like a fine one, said Mr. Lipinski, moving closer. *Will you show to me?*

William kicked off his shoes and walked into the living room. Kneeling on the floor, he unrolled the carpet. Mr. Lipinski slowly knelt beside him. *William,* he said, *this looks very zawrotny.* Nodding his head up and down.

Zawrotny?

Yes, how you say, beautiful maybe, stunning.

Yes, I thought so too. Zawrotny!

The two men smiled at each other and then looked away.

THE APARTMENT

William's apartment at the top of the house was compact and took up the entire third floor. He had his own little bathroom with a big clawfoot tub, a counter with electric burners, a toaster oven, and a small fridge. He didn't have a kitchen sink and had to wash his dishes in the bathroom. This amused William. He knew it would appall his mother and he relished the unconventionality. The room was furnished with two lovely bay windows that fronted the street. His desk was shoved up against one and his bed carefully positioned close to the other. This lay-out created two distinct areas for William: one for sleeping and one to organize his school materials. It pleased him to have two compartmentalized areas. And now he had two carpets. One of these was already laid out at the foot of his bed, infusing the room with its richness. The second carpet he rolled out behind his desk chair, creating a vibrant island of warm colour that competed for attention. William stood there contemplating his two carpets. He sighed happily, feeling dazzled by their beauty.

Then he sat down on the floor and simply stared at them by turn. He felt as though he was in possession of a great secret. *Such objects of beauty*, he thought, *with their energy and colour*. They were as seductive to him as a beautiful girl, and seemed far more enduring.

THE METHOD

William's closest friends were fellow students, and together they combatted the stress of their routine by playing squash, swimming laps, and forming "study groups" that met at any number of the small pubs around campus. Brian, one of his intimates, had decided that they should regularly visit all the pubs within walking distance of the campus and chart the availability and appeal of single females. His theory was that different groups of women would frequent certain locations. For instance, he argued, art girls frequented the Queen Mum, English majors had tea at Wymilwood, and psychology majors liked the Buttery. Strolling through the Con or hanging out on Philosopher's Walk was also a good way to look for available women. They needed to isolate the type of girl who thought dentists were sexy, or at least acceptable because of their earnings potential, and prey on those. *The only way to score is to track the right animal.* That was Brian's theory.

William went along with the rest of the guys but didn't take *the method* too seriously. He wasn't particularly interested in *more of the same*. He'd dated in high school and in undergrad, but had been unimpressed by the predictability of it: coffee or tea, a movie, dinner, longer phone calls, peeling off some of her clothes and getting worked up. Then suddenly, bam, the hammer hits: When will she see him again? When will he meet her friends? When will he come for dinner with her parents? This was inevitably followed by crying, strained telephone conversations, and finally an awkward parting.

THE THIRD CARPET

The allure of the carpets continued to draw William and captivate his interest. Day after day, he deliberately passed by the storefront with its neon *Sale Today* sign. He didn't dare go in again. His picnicking friends at the back of the shop might convince him to choose another of their wares. He wouldn't allow himself that luxury. Not yet. Not until there was something significant to mark: an occasion or celebration, maybe the end of third year. William promised himself that the day after he wrote his last exam he'd casually stroll in and *just see* if there was something that caught his eye. He wouldn't necessarily *buy* it; he'd just allow himself the pleasure of looking.

William bought his third carpet when he finished third year. Months of studying and hours of standing agonizingly alert in the clinic had begun to wear. He was committed to the course he'd chosen and believed he'd be able to do some good. He also recognized that it was a good fit for his ambitions and gifts. But this didn't mean that he always enjoyed what he was doing. The lectures were often dry, the slides shocking. The patients at the clinic mostly suffered from poor nutrition and poor oral hygiene. It often seemed bleak.

The third carpet was a silk Qum from Central Iran. A red-flowering plant grew in a riot of leaves and blossoms up the middle. The borders contained smaller versions of the plant and its flower. The colours were tantalizing. The background was ivory, the fill colours of the border a deep medium blue. But the leaves and flowers were alive with vibrant greens and reds and yellows and whites. It was his largest—four feet five inches by seven—and most expensive carpet. William knew he'd have to rearrange his room to accommodate it. The younger of the carpet masters showed him the reverse side where canvas loops had been skilfully integrated into the structure. *For hanging*, he said. *You do not want to walk on this carpet.* William was delighted.

The third carpet meant having to ask Stan Lipinski if he could drill some brackets in the wall. Stan came upstairs with his drill and helped him with the mounting.

Pointing to the carpet, William asked, *Zawrotny?*

Stan nodded and smiled at him. *Yes, zawrotny.*

It was clear that Stan didn't think William's appreciation of the carpets was eccentric. William was relieved by this. He'd never brought friends by his apartment and shown off his little collection. His parents were collectors too, but he saw their acquisitions as vulgar appropriations. When they travelled, they'd come back with suitcases filled with cheap local clothing and trinkets. His mother would display these to her friends as artifacts of her latest holiday. Eventually they'd be boxed up and moved to the basement or garage. William had no patience for that kind of collecting.

PAMELA

The Lipinskis' daughter, Pamela, was their pride and joy. William observed that although she treated her parents affectionately, she wasn't always respectful towards them. This intrigued William. His parents, particularly his father, would not have tolerated anything less than complete obedience and respect. William had learned very early that the way to have an easy life was to be a pleaser. Do what was required, when it was required, and in the required manner. Polished manners and a sense of propriety rounded out the formula. Grey flannel trousers and a navy blue blazer were the uniform of choice, along with an expensive trench coat from Stollery's and smartly polished Allen Edmunds shoes. This uniform would allow any gentleman to negotiate most social circumstances.

Pam was entirely different. She wasn't deferential and not much was required of her at home. Maria did the housework and the laundry and the meal preparation. Stan did the yard work and the maintenance. Pam seemed free to please herself, and would lounge around the house looking disdainful and pained when asked to help with anything. He supposed she was spoiled. But that didn't make sense in some ways. *He* was spoiled. *He* was the rich kid from St. Clair and Avenue Road. She had friends over occasionally, and he could hear them squealing excitedly in her bedroom. Sometimes he'd get a glimpse of them with their hair in rollers and white goop on their faces. The smell of nail polish remover and hairspray often wafted above the stairs to his room. Pam never spoke to William. She'd look down when they passed each other in the house and flatten her profile against the wall. It was as though his very presence intruded upon her domain and she would prefer not to even acknowledge him. William was fine with that. It kept things uncomplicated.

STAN AND MARIA

Stan and Maria were the perfect landlords. They didn't raise the rent, they didn't intrude, and they were sociable when he felt like company. They were good people, he thought. He began to be aware of their routines, and found himself monitoring them in an absent-minded sort of way. Thursday night was Bingo at the Hall. Saturday morning was Confession and a stop at the bakery for fresh bread and pastry. Sunday at ten was Mass. Sunday lunch was soup and roast beef. Sunday afternoon was a walk in the park. And so it went. Stan was always holding out Maria's chair or opening doors for her. He often saw them linking their arms when they went out together. William loved seeing this. Loved the idea that after a lifetime together they still cared for each other. His own parents never touched or demonstrated affection in public. Even when he was a child his father would simply shake William's hand after a good report card or news of a home run. He couldn't remember ever being swooped up in a giant bear hug or carried around on piggyback. That just didn't happen in his family.

ANNA'S

Fourth year was spent almost entirely at the clinic. There were still lectures and assignments and many levels of exams, but the focus was on clinical training. William found the technical aspects of dentistry easier to manage than the interpersonal ones. He didn't like to inflict pain. He didn't have an easy manner that instilled calm in frightened patients. He watched his friends tackle case after case seemingly without emotional involvement. William envied them their ability to disassociate themselves from the task at hand. He decided that two additional years of specialization would allow him to focus on work that corrected people's teeth rather than spending a lifetime doing overdue checkups, fillings, and extractions. He would be an orthodontist. His parents were pleased with his decision—it was better, at least, than being a mere dentist—and extended his generous living allowance. The Lipinskis were happy to have William stay with them a further two years. He was a respectable young man on his way up in the world.

In year five, William started eating his Sunday night meal at a little local restaurant called Anna's. It wasn't fancy but served hearty Polish and Hungarian food in generous portions. The staff were friendly and didn't mind if he spread his books out across the table and lingered to study after his meal. William loved the familiar setting that still provided some anonymity. It was a perfect balance for him. He looked forward to his weekly forays and went for long walks afterwards to help digest the rich fare.

To his surprise one night, Pam arrived beside his table, swathed in an overlarge white apron and poised to take his order. *Pam?*

She looked down at the floor. *Yes. I'm finished school now and must work. This is a good job.*

Yes, of course it is. I was just surprised to see you.

At first William was uncomfortable with her there. She was an intrusion into his sanctuary, a piece that didn't quite fit. But he had no choice: he had to adapt or find another place for his Sunday meal. The first couple of weeks he'd pack up his books at closing time and begin his evening walk. But then one night, as he approached the street where he lived, he saw Pam ahead of him, walking home in the dark. This concerned him. The neighbourhood was safe during the day, but at night teenagers would often get drunk or silly and create havoc in the streets. William didn't think it was safe for her to walk alone. He began to fret about this.

The following Sunday night, instead of taking his regular evening stroll, he asked Pam if she'd like him to walk her home. She didn't answer, but at closing time, as he was packing up his books, she stood by the door in her coat waiting for him. They walked home in silence, neither of them comfortable with the other or having anything to say that would sustain conversation. William tried to find something in common, but he couldn't think of a single thing. Instead he paced silently beside her, fulfilling the role of unwilling guardian and mildly resenting the twist in his routine.

Later that week, Stan approached him. *Thank you for doing us this service. She is a stubborn girl and will not allow me to come for her.*

William was pleased that his act of selflessness had not gone unnoticed. And he was glad that Stan was happy with him. But this created a new dilemma for William. It locked him in. He had no choice now but to continue escorting Pam home after her shift on Sunday nights. Failure to do so might be taken as disrespectful to the Lipinskis, and he didn't want to do anything they might regard as a slight.

Gradually, over the following weeks, Pam began to dart quick glances at him when she took his order. She even made suggestions about the daily specials. Sometimes, when he was later than usual, he'd notice that "his" table had been reserved for him, the chairs tipped up in expectation of his arrival. That small act gladdened him. It made him feel that, in some small way, he was significant and that it mattered to someone what he ate for Sunday dinner. As was his habit, William continued to tip generously for monopolizing one of the tables all evening. One night, Pam brought him his change and said, *You shouldn't pay so much. It's too much.* William was touched by this.

He was chatty on the way home that night. He told her about his studies and his work at the clinic. He told her about his friends and some of the stupid stunts they pulled on each other. Although she seemed interested, and laughed at the appropriate times, Pam didn't contribute much to the conversation. William attributed this to shyness and a lack of experience with men. He found it endearing. While opening the door for her that evening, his arm inadvertently grazed Pam's hip. He apologized and stepped back to allow her to pass through into the house. Before moving forward, Pam turned and looked at him full in the face. It was the first time she'd looked directly at him. He noticed that her eyeliner was smeared a little in the corners, that her lipstick was worn off, and more than that, that she looked tired. Her big green eyes stared at him boldly and took in his measure. He blushed under the scrutiny.

OBSESSION

The desire to touch her became an obsession for William. It came over him suddenly and did not dissipate. It was an intense animal attraction that simply gnawed at him. Her thin childlike arms, her large emerald eyes, her shapely hips and softly rounded bottom, the suggestion of warm breasts concealed beneath the thin cotton blouses she wore. He could not rationalize away these urges no matter how hard he tried. She had become an idée fixe and he was suddenly smitten. Sunday nights became the pinnacle of his week. He dressed carefully for his dinners. He used mouthwash, he polished his shoes. He saved up conversational tidbits that he could use on the walk home. He gave himself stern talks about the difference in their ages, their lack of commonalities, the gap in education. He envisioned taking her to meet his parents and their subsequent displeasure. It seemed hopeless.

And then, abruptly, one Saturday morning everything changed. He heard the door shutting early in the morning when the Lipinskis left for church and their bakery run. He ran the tub for his bath and settled in for a leisurely start to the day. Wrapped in a towel, he emerged from the bathroom to find Pam seated cross-legged on one of his carpets. The Herati. She was wearing pink pyjamas. Thin cotton pyjamas with little strawberries. He stood there staring at her. *I wanted to see the carpets,* she said softly. *I heard my father talking about them. Do you mind?*

No, of course not. But he was distracted by her bare feet, with bright pink nail polish carefully applied on each of the shapely little toes. *How could she have such beautiful feet,* William wondered, *without my ever knowing it?*

Show me, she said, *what you love about them.* She stood up at that and moved towards the silk Qum mounted on the wall. She reached out tentatively to touch it but stopped herself, looking at William for permission.

Go ahead, you can touch. It won't hurt.

It's so smooth, she said while brushing her hands gently across the surface.

Gripping the towel he was wrapped in, William walked over, and standing just slightly behind her, pointed to the intricate border. *Look at the detail in those small flowers,* he said, inhaling the fragrance of her shampoo. *Can you imagine the time it took to make each of those small knots?*

Show me. What else?

William pointed to a detail in the leaves that had always moved him, a curling of the tip of a leaf with a slight change in colour. *It's so carefully done. I can't imagine a more exquisite treatment.*

Pam leaned forward and peered at the leaf tip. The light from his window illuminated her profile and perfectly highlighted her body through the thin fabric of her pyjamas. William felt himself going hard. He tensed his glutes, he sucked in his stomach muscles, he tried to will himself away from her.

William? she said, looking directly into his eyes while moving closer.

Yes?

By way of reply, Pam unbuttoned her pyjama top and let it fall to the floor. Then she loosened her bottoms and stepped out of them, kicking them aside. William dropped his towel as he reached for her.

She came to his room Saturday mornings for the next three weeks. He'd lie in bed waiting to hear the Lipinskis leave. Then, quietly, he heard her feet on the stairs. She burst into his room and stripped off her clothes quickly. He folded back the covers and she slipped into bed with him. They never spoke during these interludes; they only ever touched and explored the secrets of each other's bodies. Conversations were restricted to their walks home together on Sunday nights. But even then they wouldn't talk of their physical trysts, only about the mundane. William disciplined himself not to grab at her in the halls or speak to her in the house. Like every other aspect of William's schedule, his involvement with Pam was neatly timetabled.

SPOILED GOODS

It ended one Saturday when, having lost a sense of time, they fell asleep in William's bathtub. They heard the door opening downstairs and this roused them suddenly. William threw on his clothes as Pam struggled into her pyjamas. Maria was on the stairs calling to her. She saw Pam descend from the third floor, wet and sleepy, her top undone. Maria shrieked. William waited for the shouting to stop before he went downstairs. Stan was pacing in the dining room.

William expected to be told to leave immediately. He braced himself. Instead, Stan said, *Do you love her?*

William was unprepared for this question. Stan asked again, *Do you love her?*

Yes. I suppose so.

No. You do not suppose to love. You do or you don't.

William was devastated by such a reproach.

She is ruined now, spoiled goods. It was for her to be careful. She is foolish.

I'll marry her, let me marry her. The words surprised William as much as they did Stan. He couldn't believe they had actually come from his own mouth. But he'd said them and he would honour them. He would do the right thing.

No. Marriage is hard enough for two people who love each other. You are not a match. Your parents would not agree to this. There is no love. I cannot allow it.

Stan left William alone in the dining room. When William stood up to return to his apartment, he saw that Maria was in the kitchen with her apron over her head, sobbing. He climbed the stairs and paused on the second-floor landing. From the direction of Pam's room, he heard angry voices. Stan was chastising her. William deliberated going down the hall and proposing to her gallantly but did not think Stan would appreciate this. Feeling helpless and miserable, William packed his schoolbooks and a few personal things in an overnight bag. He would go home for a few days to let things cool down.

ENGAGED

William returned to the Indian Grove house a couple of weeks later. He hadn't called or stopped by. He'd decided to find another place. He would leave cheques for the next three months and simply return to the apartment and clear out his clothes and the carpets. Everything else could stay for the next tenant. He timed his visit to coincide with the Lipinskis' return from the bakery. He wouldn't sneak in and out like a thief, nor would he seek out Pam. Unsure of how best to approach the matter, he waited on the front porch.

Stan didn't seem surprised to see him. *William, you are well?*

Yes, sir. Well enough. Busy at school.

Come, beckoned Stan, *we should talk.* Maria shuffled past William without acknowledging him. William followed Stan into the dining room and stood waiting for him to say something.

Maybe we should go to the park? offered Stan. *I like to walk there when I think.*

William nodded his agreement and followed Stan back outside. *I need to apologize, sir, for what happened. I want you to know that I plan to move out this week.*

If this is what you want, William.

It's the right thing to do, sir.

Maybe yes, maybe no. It's as you want. Pam is sad. She is . . . He paused and began again. *Pam is . . .* But the old man was choked up and could not finish his sentence. William looked at him and saw that Stan was crying. Fat tears were spilling down his weathered face. He looked devastated.

William had never seen his own father cry. He knew that men did cry, but he'd had no experience with it. Seeing Stan in this state upset him. He wasn't sure if he actually loved Pam, but he was sure that he respected Stan and didn't want to disappoint him. It was a family bond that William wanted—acceptance and kindness and generosity. *Pam is what, Stan? You must tell me.*

To be a mother . . .

Shit! Are you sure?

Yes. Stan nodded sadly. *We are sure.*

William's parents were less than impressed when he told them the news. *You don't have to marry her,* said his father. *We can make a settlement. I'll call Douglas at the firm. Don't be stupid and throw your life away on some cheap Polack.*

I really liked Louise from the club, said his mother. *Why don't you marry a nice girl like Louise?*

While William was exasperated by them, he also understood their anxiety. *She's carrying my child. I won't walk away from my own blood.*

THE WHEELERS

Stella didn't know her father's parents very well. They lived in Myrtle Beach for six months of the year and at their cottage on Lake Joseph for three. Otherwise they either travelled or were at their condo on the edge of Old Thornhill. William had stipulated a minimum of four visits per year: one week in July at the cottage, Thanksgiving in Thornhill, a May weekend in Waldham, a birthday visit for Stella. They didn't celebrate Christmas or holidays together. An envelope filled with cash was the only gift Stella ever remembered receiving from them.

The contrast between her two sets of grandparents had always interested her. Her father's parents, so busy, so elegantly dressed, were formal with their son and offhand with Stella. They would stare at her with curiosity at the beginning of their quarterly family times but then seem to forget her. The Lipinskis, on the other hand, were always affectionate and welcoming, never satisfied with either the length or the frequency of their get-togethers. They focused intently on all three of their *dzieci,* fussing over each with special interest and pride. As a child, Stella would bring them crayoned pictures and later her tests and assignments to show them how well she was doing in school. These treasures were proudly displayed on the fridge door for all to see.

The Lipinskis

Grandfather Lipinski was Stella's favourite grandparent. He was entirely different from anyone else in her life. He seemed to live for those precious moments when Stella would emerge from the car and run into his open arms. When she was small he would clasp her tightly in a bear hug, but as she became more developed he demonstrated restraint and would hug her only lightly, as though she had become a fragile thing, holding her for mere seconds before releasing her to seek out her grandmother, who always had a plate of cookies waiting at the kitchen table.

Her grandfather typically wore a V-necked sweater, even in the summer. Usually it was in a dark tone, grey or navy blue or brown. Under that he wore plaid shirts in sombre earth colours, and under that a white undershirt that peeked through the opening of his collar. Grandmother always wore a flowered dress with a large patterned apron. The colours and prints clashed, and this was something that Stella noticed. She knew it wasn't important and that it *shouldn't* matter to her, but somehow, *it did.*

As a child, each visit always included a small *tchotchke* or treat for Stella. Sometimes it was a walk to the park to see the zoo and eat roasted chestnuts, with her grandfather carefully peeling the blackened shell and passing her the tender nutmeat. At other times it was a trip to the bakery to smell the fresh bread and buy a piece of poppyseed strudel. Often it would be a very special gift: a robin's egg blown hollow, a peacock feather, a new pencil with a shiny painted coating in bright purple or pink. Thoughtful, magical things.

The house was a dark, fortress-like, three-storey red-brick building with wrought-iron bars on the basement windows. There was a metal roller blind that pulled down over the front picture window and locked from the inside. All the shutters were on working hinges, and these could be swung closed against the panes of glass and secured. The front and back doors had dead-bolts and safety chains and pins that fastened to the floor. Stella sensed, even as a child, that these security measures were meant to protect the occupants. She did not finger the locks or play with the shutters. Somehow she knew, without ever being told, that this would create anxiety for her grandparents.

The security wasn't the only unusual thing to Stella. In the basement was a big cold room that had been constructed from concrete blocks. The walls were lined with metal shelves that went from floor to ceiling. In this room were sleeping bags, large jugs of water, flashlights with packages of batteries, an old-fashioned transistor radio, a Coleman stove with cylinders of propane, first aid supplies, and many, many tins of food. The array of tins was staggering. It was like having a private grocery store in the basement. When her grandparents went shopping, using their metal bundle buggy and walking to the local Dominion, they bought two of everything. The two new items would be carried downstairs and rotated carefully with two older tins. In this way, their stock was constantly replenished.

Nothing was ever wasted in this house. String was unknotted and wound around sticks. Paper clips and thumbtacks and safety pins were saved in empty glass jars. Elastic bands were stretched and added to a rubber ball made entirely of elastics. Buttons and zippers from worn out, discarded clothing were kept in big cookie tins. Tinfoil was washed and reused until it began to perish. Paper bags were ironed and saved in a kitchen drawer. Stella's father told her that their many years of deprivation during the war had led them to value each little thing they owned and taught them to be careful. Her mother dismissed their habits as crazy and was ashamed of their eccentricities.

Grandfather Lipinski also did not trust banks. *If there is a war*, he would say, *the government will seize your money and you will be left with nothing*. He'd developed his own banking system. Empty pickle jars were filled with spare change and hidden in the basement rafters. Folding money was rolled up tightly with an elastic band and stored in jam jars. In some ways, it was an efficient method. And yet her father worried about them. Worried that they'd be robbed or that the house might catch fire and they'd lose everything. He tried repeatedly to convince her grandfather to invest at least *some* of the money in a bank. Stan humoured William by opening a small account in the DUCA, a Dutch credit union, located a long subway and bus ride away.

Stan, William would begin, *I have a friend at the Bank of Nova Scotia. He's a good man. I trust him . . .*

But these conversations would go nowhere. Her father would mutter good-naturedly about the old man's stubborn streak in the car on the way home to Waldham. Stella knew that her father was fond of Grandfather Lipinski and that he took a genuine interest in his well-being. He continued, even after leaving Pam, to call Stella up and ask if she'd like him to visit the Lipinskis with her. He'd arrive in his black Mercedes and drive her to the house, where he'd open the trunk and grin at her while unpacking baskets of fruit and cheese, a bouquet of freshly cut flowers, a bottle of schnapps. These offerings were received in stony silence and, once they were stowed away, did not make a further appearance.

Although her grandparents were none too pleased with their son-in-law for the divorce, they were happy to see his continued interest in Stella and didn't want to discourage his visits with her. This state of détente infuriated Pamela, who sulked for weeks when she discovered that her parents were complicit with the visits. After a year of such politely stiff encounters, Grandfather Lipinski began to actually open the schnapps and share a little drink, *for old times' sake*, before William and Stella had to leave. Eventually, Grandpa Lipinski appeared to forget entirely that he was supposed to be angry with William and began to shake his hand when he arrived and pat him convivially on the back when he was leaving. Grandma Lipinski was not as enthusiastic, but she began to set the table with four places and managed to prepare fresh cabbage rolls or latkes or perogies when she knew they were coming.

Whether her grandparents had forgotten about her father's misdeeds was something that Stella speculated about but did not ask. It didn't seem possible that they could so easily ignore the fact that their daughter had been displaced. But then, Stella reasoned, they had witnessed far worse in their lives. Somehow their life experiences had given them the ability to see grey in a world where her mother saw only black and white.

BOY SCOUTS

Grandfather Lipinski once told Stella and William that at the start of the war, in 1939, he'd been digging ditches with a group of boy scouts when a Russian truck pulled up and armed soldiers forced them to get in. They boys were driven for three days across Ukraine to a work camp. His first winter there was spent in the forest cutting lumber. Without any outdoor clothing he suffered severe frostbite on his ears, and for the rest of his life they would swell up red whenever the temperature dropped below freezing. Stella had seen this herself after a long winter walk in High Park. The pain would come back then too, Stan said; he'd have to hold his hands to his ears and rub them until the stinging stopped.

Stella's father chimed in then, telling Stella that the Russians had executed thousands of Polish officers as well as many boy scouts in the work camps. The Russians blamed the Nazis. The Germans blamed the Russians. Mass graves continued to be uncovered. Grandfather Lipinski said that the officers would pull down the boys' pants to see whether they were circumcised. The Jewish boys were put in one truck and the non-Jews in another. Her grandpa was put on the non-Jewish truck.

In his second year of internment, he told her, he volunteered to work inside the camp with a tailor making army uniforms. He pretended to know how to operate a sewing machine. The tailor saw that he'd lied and quickly taught him the basics. The kindly man had simply said, *You are too young to freeze to death*.

In 1942 there was talk in the camp of the Americans, who had entered the war by then and were now fighting alongside Britain. Hopeful whispers spread. The young began to take heart, to believe their nightmare might soon be ended. They thought the end of the war would happen quickly—Germans and Russians were fighting along the Eastern Front and there was talk of many casualties. But the tailor was frightened. He told Stan that the Germans were crazy. They wanted Ukraine for its food and would stop at nothing to win. *If they come here*, said the tailor, *we will all be killed*.

At night, in the wooden barracks, Stan slept on a slatted bed with no straw and no covers. He had only his thin cotton scout uniform and a pair of worn boots. Everything was filthy and his skin was covered in crusty patches and sores. His hair was falling out from malnourishment. *God is good*, Stan would say to himself. *There must be more for me than this*. He prayed for deliverance through the Americans.

One day the tailor said, *Stanislaw, tonight you must make your escape. Under the fence, you must crawl. Hide in the latrines until it is dark and still. If it is cloudy tonight, and no stars, you should go. Take others with you. The Germans are getting closer. This will be your last chance. Take this*. The tailor passed him a heel of bread and a couple of potato pieces. *My food from yesterday*.

And so Stan escaped with three other young men, all of them in their early twenties. They hid in the forest. They'd cut wood there and knew the paths, and so they fled through the forest under cover of darkness until they were farther than they'd ever been, their chests hurting from the running and the cold air. It wasn't until the sun began to rise that they burrowed into little hillocks of snow, trying to make themselves invisible. They wept silently and slept in the freezing hole they'd made until there was no feeling left in their fingers or toes and they wanted never to waken. For eight days they wandered and hid in the forest, unsure of their direction, dazed by the cold and hunger, frightened of capture.

Then one day they heard the sounds of a battle. Gunfire. Unending hours of gunfire. All through the day and all through the night they heard the sounds. They argued among themselves about what to do. *What if it's the Russians?* they asked each other. *They'll kill us for sure. What if it's the Germans?* they asked. *They'll kill us too. But it could be the Americans,* they said. *They could liberate us.*

And because they were starving and stupefied by frostbite and fear, they moved towards the gunfire and prepared to meet their fate. *Better to be shot than to spend more time starving in the cold,* they reasoned. With their arms in the air, they ran towards the soldiers and prayed they were Americans. They were not. The boys were seized immediately and tied together. Then they were taken to a Red Cross tent and fed spoonfuls of warm broth. For days afterwards they were interrogated. Were they Polish subversives? Were they Russians? How could they have escaped from the camp? How could they have survived for so long in the forest? Had someone helped them?

Finally, thankfully, the field marshal believed them—maybe because they all said the same thing over and over again or maybe because they were such pathetic figures. Leaning over an unsteady camp table, they signed long handwritten affidavits and agreed to enlist with the British. They were transported to England for basic training; later, Stan and one of his friends, Maciej, were chosen to go to Scotland for armoured vehicle training. Six months after that he and Maciej were sent to the Netherlands, where heavy fighting raged between the Allies and the Germans. Stan was the driver in a Sherman tank division with a small crew of five. Maciej was a gunner.

MACIEJ

One evening Stan decided to bed down under a tree. It was summer, and he desperately wanted some fresh air. All those days in a hot tank—when you couldn't breathe, when your lungs had so much pressure that you could never catch your breath properly—those days were hard, and he craved deep breaths in the open air. Maciej wanted to be outside as well, but to be safe he dug a small hole under one of the two tanks and slept there. They called out to each other quietly before submitting to their weariness.

In the night, Stan woke suddenly to the sound of a Stuka screaming—a terrible noise that made your blood run cold and your body sweat at the same time. Bright lights and a heavy thud and the earth shook. A confusion of sounds and fire. The two parked tanks had been hit. The explosion happened fifty feet from where Stan had lain sleeping. He shouted Maciej's name and ran over to the tank, but there was only fire with parts of the tanks thrown all around. The metal was burning. Stan fell to the ground and sobbed, pounding the earth. The dirt itself was hot. Red Cross workers found him there two days later. He had severe burns on his hands from lifting the hot metal and sifting through the wreckage, looking for his friend. He was the only survivor from the two crews. One in ten. A rescue worker told him he was lucky. *Lucky,* he thought. *Maciej is dead. How is that luck?*

Stella had heard the story several times in her growing-up years. She always wept silently, reaching up with the palm of her hand to blot away the streaming tears. She wept for the young man who had died so needlessly and wept for her grandfather who had lost the last person he loved and felt connected to. And she wept to think of such savage loss.

THE VISIT

When Stella was in university she'd often take the subway to her grandparents' house for a visit and a hot meal. She tried to do this at least once a week during the term, before she had to study for her exams. Her grandmother wasn't a very good telephone conversationalist, but it was she who always picked up the ringing phone. *Hello, who is this?* was her shouted greeting, a tinge of panic in her voice. She was uncomfortable speaking with someone she couldn't see or easily identify.

It's me, Grandma, how are you?

Fine.

Would it be all right if I came by for a visit tomorrow?

You'll stay for dinner?

Yes, if you'll have me.

Yes!

I'll see you tomorrow then, Grandma.

When Stella would arrive the following afternoon, she'd find the dining room table beautifully set with a lace tablecloth and the good china and silver. She felt like a special guest. Dinner would be a soup course and a main course and dessert. There was always soup, even in the summer, and it invariably consisted of hearty chunks of turnip and carrots and potatoes and onion with shredded cabbage and bits of meat spiced heavily with black pepper. The main course might be a stew or perogies or a pork roast with vegetables. Dessert was pastry or piece of strudel from the bakery. Grandpa would have bought *something nice* in the morning while out for his daily walk.

One afternoon she arrived at the house and knocked at the side door. When her grandmother came to let her in, Stella saw at once that Maria had a flushed face and had been crying. *Are you okay?*

Maria directed her to the living room. They never sat there; it was for company. With the exception of Christmas, Stella had never been invited into the room. Her mother always complained that, although it was furnished in French provincial furniture with fruitwood tables and brass lamps, her grandparents kept the room draped in sheets.

Ma, Pam would say, *do you think the furniture is going to improve with age? It's not an art gallery. Why not look at it once in a while?*

It's good to be careful with such things, her mother would respond. Sometimes she spoke to Pamela in Polish, but Pam would cut her off abruptly. *In English, Ma.*

Pam's distaste for her parents' idiosyncrasies was evident to Stella at an early age. Sometimes her father, when he was still living with them, would check Pam and ask her to be gentler with them.

They're my parents, she would snap. *I think I know how to talk to my own parents.*

But they've been through so much, her husband would counter. *A little kindness would go a long way.*

Stella thought of this conversation years later. She wondered if her father's concern was an expression of more than what he'd actually said. Was this a crack in his veneer? Was it the beginning of his *other interests*?

Now Stella walked into the living room and saw her grandfather on the draped couch, holding his stomach and rocking back and forth. She crossed the room and knelt before him. *Grandpa, what's wrong? Are you sick?*

He reached for her with one hand and stopped the rocking motion. His hand rested on the top of her shoulder. He didn't speak. He looked dazed. His complexion was grey. He was panting slightly. *Grandpa, are you in pain? Shall I call a cab? Take you to the hospital?*

There was no response. She rifled through her purse, took out her cell phone, and began to stand. Her grandfather's hand gripped her arm. She looked down at him. *Call your father.*

WILLIAM AND STAN

*D*ad, I'm at Grandpa's and he's not well. I think I have to take him to the hospital but he wanted me to call you.
Put him on the phone.

Stella sat beside her grandfather and placed the phone by his ear. *Stan,* she heard her father call. *Stan, it's William. Are you okay, Stan? Do you need Stella to take you to the hospital?*

No hospital, just you.

It'll take me an hour to get there. Are you sure you can wait?

Yes.

Stella took the phone and spoke to William. *What should I do?*

Sit with him, and watch carefully. If he has trouble breathing, call 911. I'll leave right away.

Stella shut the phone and put her arms around her grandfather. He didn't respond and together they sat like that, linked in a one-sided embrace. Soon Maria came in and motioned to Stella. Reluctantly, she got up and followed her to the kitchen.

Is your father coming?

Yes, he'll be here in an hour. What happened?

He was out walking and he saw someone. He came home scared. It's good that your father is coming. He will talk to him.

Is he okay?

Yes, luby, he will be okay. Maria didn't sound convincing. She too looked worried and upset. Stella went back into the living room, where Stan had resumed rocking in his place on the couch. She turned on the overhead light, sat down quietly beside him, and waited.

MOERDIJK

At the sound of a car in the driveway, Stella sprang up and ran to the door. When her father rushed in she pointed silently at the living room and he strode on through. He stood in front of Stan, picking up his wrist and holding it in his hand to check the pulse. Then he bent over and gently tipped Stan's chin upwards so that he could look into his eyes. Finally, he felt his forehead.

Stan, what happened? Are you all right? Do you want me to take you to the hospital?

Her grandfather looked up at him and shook his head. *I saw him. I saw him, and he saw me.*

Saw who? Who did you see?

Maria came in and stood beside Stella, who reached for her hand.

I saw his eyes. They all waited for him to continue. The room was silent. *It was him. Those eyes you don't mistake.*

Who, Stan? asked William again. *Who was it?*

A Nazi dog!

Stella shuddered. Goosebumps formed on her arms and she felt a chill on the back of her neck. Her grandma squeezed her hand tightly.

Tell me, said her father, speaking calmly. *Tell me what you saw.*

In the park, feeding ducks. I thought, how nice. I watched him. His hand went into the bag of breadcrumbs and came out. He threw the crumbs on the lake. His arm did not bend so good. I watched. Again he put his hand in the bag and pulled it out. He threw the crumbs. And then I knew. I felt it. I was shaking. He felt it. He turned and looked at me and he made a face. A terrible face. A face with hatred. We stared at each other. He walked away very fast. I could not walk. I felt sick.

Are you all right? asked William. *Do you need a glass of water?* Her father looked at Stella and she understood. She went to the kitchen and returned with a big glass of cold tap water. William held it to her grandfather's lips and helped him drink. Then he placed the glass on the draped fruitwood table. No coaster. Stella watched the moisture wick from the glass onto the sheet. It would mark the table. She didn't move. No one else seemed to notice. *It would be wrong,* she thought, *to trouble about such a thing at a time like this.*

We were on a one-night leave near Moerdijk in 1944, began her grandfather. *All of us. There was dancing in a small place. It was one night. We drank a little beer and we danced a little. The Dutch girls were friendly to us. We had defeated the Germans in Breda and we felt happy. We thought the worst was over.*

Go on, encouraged her father. *Get it all out, Stan. It's okay.*

He nodded and continued. His hands were braced on his knees. His knees were shaking. William reached across and placed his own hands on top of the old man's, gently steadying his limbs.

It was nighttime. We were walking back to our camp when we saw the planes dropping paratroopers. Junkers, J52s. Soon the sky was filled with planes and men dropping down. We knew who it was. All around the countryside we could see hundreds of men dropping from the sky. We didn't know what to do. We were not armed. We ran back to the village and told the Dutch. They hid us in a small kelder. A tiny room half in the ground. They pushed something heavy in front of the door. We squeezed together. The Dutch ran away to their houses.

Grandpa paused. Stella watched him and watched her father tending him. His gentleness moved her. She felt spellbound. Maria was now seated in a chair, weeping quietly, her hands twisting the fabric of her apron. Stella was trembling. William was the only one in control.

We stayed there overnight. We slept standing up. There was nowhere to piss. We didn't talk. Through a crack beside the door we saw a little light. That was all. The next day there was noise. The door was banged open with something hard. Boots marched across the floor. We closed our eyes and held our breathing. The sound of a child came too. Crying. I was close to the crack and I opened my eyes to look. There was a girl on the floor with a Nazi on top of her and another one waiting for his turn. They used her and when they were done, they shot her. The sound was so loud. Then they left. We waited until night and we crept out. We covered her. She was very young.

William spoke first. *Stan, you can't be sure it was the same man. You were in a closet.*

It was him. I saw. His arm was the same. The elbow works both ways. I saw. You don't forget such an evil. I was in the right place to see.

Would you like me to call the police?

Pah! The police. What do they know about it? They know nothing.

We should tell someone, Stella offered. *I'm sure there's someone who tracks war criminals. They extradite them.*

No! We do nothing. I do not want people knowing where we live. We tell no one.

QUESTIONS

That night in bed, Stella began to turn things over in her mind. There were pieces missing in her grandfather's story, and things she couldn't reconcile. Why, if there was a group of Polish soldiers hidden in the closet, had they not tried to overpower the two Nazis raping the Dutch girl? And the bond between Stan and William: Why had her father continued to visit his former in-laws and why did her grandparents still treat him like a son? Why had they wanted only him when they were frightened and upset? And why had they so quickly dismissed the idea of the police?

VISIT HOME

Stella cocooned herself in her dorm room and read her course texts obsessively. At other times she'd burrow into a study carrel at Robarts Library and pile stacks of books around her, walling herself away. She didn't call home or speak to her grandparents or her father. It was as though she'd been made privy to a shameful secret, and it left her feeling somehow soiled and inadequate. If she called William he'd ask after Stan and Maria, which would fill her with guilt and require a complex response he might consider uncaring. She didn't know how to have a conversation with Pam about such things. Would she be shocked by the Nazi in the park, or would she just complain how *she'd* been traumatized by her parents' obsession with all things war-related? And so Stella found herself in a kind of stasis. Words didn't come easily to her in situations involving emotional matters. She did not possess the gift of saying *just the right thing*.

Her mother was typically never any help in this regard. Pam's responses were always Pam-centric. *If we're not talking about me, then why are we talking?* was how Stella's closest friend, Tara Putsey, described her. There was, unfortunately, much truth to this cruel summation. Pam *was* self-absorbed.

When Stella arrived home on Saturday morning with a pillowcase filled with laundry and a backpack full of books, her mother greeted her with *I hope you've had lunch already because there's nothing in the house to feed you.*

This, Stella knew, was her cue to take Pam grocery shopping in the old Ford Taurus, parked for weeks at a time in their garage. Although Pam had a driver's licence, she preferred to be driven. She routinely saved her errands for Stella's biweekly visits home, and then would press her into chauffeuring her to the hairdresser's, the bank, Hayford's Dry Goods & Department Store. Any impatience on Stella's part was met with a tirade about her ingratitude for the sacrifices Pam had made to *give her everything*.

Give her everything was one of Pam's themes. It meant she'd sacrificed her own goals and dreams to stay home with Stella in Waldham. Stella had once asked her what these goals and dreams actually were. Indignant, stony silence. They'd spent the rest of that weekend not speaking and Stella had returned to Victoria College in disgrace, her mother refusing even to kiss her good-bye. Stella would not make that mistake again.

The next weekend Stella stopped to grocery-shop first. She wouldn't likely get all the things her mother needed, but it might at least postpone all the usual back-and-forth, across-town driving.

Hi Mom, I'm home, she called out. *I picked up some shopping first. You okay?* Stella walked to the kitchen to unpack the canvas bags.

Why didn't you call first? Pam appeared in the doorway wrapped in a black velour dressing gown. *There were some things I might have wanted. You could have asked.*

Stella stepped towards her and kissed her cheek. *I know, Mom, I can go out again later. I just thought I'd pick up the basics first.*

Okay, but it seems like a lot of extra trips.

What are we doing today? Did you want to go out?

No, my arms hurt and I didn't sleep a wink all night. I ache all over. I couldn't even get dressed this morning.

I'm sorry. Do you want me to get you anything? A cup of tea?

I just have to go lie down.

What if I bring you a nice snack? I picked up some fresh pastries.

Pam moved to inspect the proffered Danish. *I'll have the raspberry one, toasted with butter.*

Okay, you lie down and I'll bring it.

Pam left the kitchen holding her hand to the small of her back and taking slow baby steps down the carpeted hallway. Stella watched quietly as she walked away.

PAM AND STELLA

As the Danish warmed in the toaster oven, Stella saw that the first of the leaves had come down in the back garden and would need raking. She stood at the sink, gazing out the window, and sighed. Then, when the Danish was ready, she wheeled the trolley down the deep-carpeted hall to what had been her father's at-home office but was now her mother's room. The built-in bookshelves that had once housed journals and university texts now displayed Royal Doulton figurines, a collection that had been amassed over her parents' nineteen-year marriage. Her father had selected them, Stella realized, in a subtle attempt to interest her mother in history: Anne Boleyn, Queen Elizabeth II Coronation, Queen Victoria and Prince Albert, Mary Queen of Scots. There were others, too—Elizabeth Bennet, the Balloon Lady, a Highland Dancer—but none of the silly ones in large hats and frivolous dresses. Ironically, Stella mused, these were the ones that would have held real appeal for her mother.

Stella had often reflected on how this collection epitomized what likely went wrong in her parents' marriage. Her father had chosen the historical figures and iconographic pieces in a futile attempt to seduce Pam into opening up her world view, but Pam valued them only as acquisitions that demonstrated their comfortable financial state. She displayed them proudly on their little wooden bases and stacked the satin-lined boxes in neat rows along the lower bookshelves. The only exceptions to this protocol were Lady Diana Spencer and HRH The Prince of Wales: an entire shelf had been dedicated to them, along with their opened boxes and documentations of authenticity. Once, just after Charles and Diana officially separated, Stella had moved the Diana figurine to the top shelf and positioned it alongside Anne Boleyn. Her mother didn't think it was funny. She cautioned Stella not to touch the figurines *ever again*.

During the later years before her father left, these carefully selected figurines had done little to break the hold of the romance novels Pam read and the soap operas she followed every afternoon. At dinner, when William would ask *What's new?*, she would begin to talk about the characters in one of her soap operas as though they were living beings and now a part of their extended family.

Her mother was in bed now, under the covers and with the curtains closed. *Mom, tea is ready.*

Pam sat up stiffly, in obvious discomfort. Stella went to her side and arranged the pillows so that she could recline against them. Pushing the trolley next to the bed, she sat down and watched as her mother sipped her tea.

I'm in so much pain today, Pam began. *You have no idea how much pain I'm in.*

Should I call the doctor? Maybe your meds need adjusting?

He won't be in today. I'll call Monday.

Is there anything I can get you?

Just sit with me. I get so lonely in this empty house.

I thought maybe I should rake some leaves today.

Why? There's more to fall. Next week there'll be twice as many. And the neighbours' blow over here too.

I can do it next week, if you want. Stella waited but there was no response from her mother. She was eating the pastry, nibbling it around the edges and saving the jam-filled bit for last. *I saw Grandma and Grandpa last week. Did they tell you?*

No, they never call me.

Well, I think Grandpa was a little upset.

Why?

He was out walking and he thought he saw someone he knew from the war. A Nazi, maybe. Stella watched her mother for a response.

He's an old fool. There's no Nazis left. He's just paranoid.

Well, I don't know, he seemed pretty upset.

You didn't encourage him, did you?

It wasn't my fault. I wasn't there. I just saw him afterwards. I thought he was sick.

Sick? How? What was wrong?

I thought maybe he was having a heart attack. I was scared.

What did you do?

I called Dad and he came.

What did you call him for? You should have just called 911. Why did you call your father?

Grandpa asked for him. He wanted to talk to him.

That makes no sense. You should have called me. I'm his daughter. It was my place to be there, not your father's. Don't you know any better by now? Pam put the last of the pastry on the plate and pushed away the trolley. She straightened the covers over her legs and looked at Stella scornfully.

He's an old fool who sees Nazis everywhere. When I was growing up he was completely paranoid. He put those bars on the basement windows and that metal blind on the front window. The house was like a fortress at night. He wouldn't go to sleep unless everything was all locked up. And we always had to leave the hall light on. He was afraid of the dark.

Mom, he lived through a terrible time.

I lived through a terrible time! Do you have any idea what it was like to grow up like that? Under the shadow of the Holocaust. Every conversation about how lucky I was. Every occasion ruined by a memory of somebody dead. We couldn't even watch the news at night without him talking about how much worse it all was then. I was sick to death of it all. I couldn't wait to leave.

That's a terrible thing to say. Are you telling me that's why you got married? To get away from Grandpa?

Not from Grandpa. From his stupid stories. The only reason he even liked your father was that he'd sit and listen to him. They'd talk for hours.

But you should be glad Grandpa had someone to talk to. Dad loves him.

Stella, don't you know anything? Your father doesn't love him. He's just a curiosity. Your father studies him. Like he does his damn rugs.

That's an awful thing to say! I don't believe you.

Believe what you want. I don't care. I have a headache. I'm going to sleep now. At that, her mother slid down in the bed and pulled the covers over her head, turning her back to Stella.

THE WHEELERS

Geoffrey and Julie Wheeler were, by all accounts, a couple who lived comfortably, entertained beautifully, were gracious guests, and understood the importance of maintaining appearances. Geoffrey sat on many boards and was well reimbursed for his business acumen. Julie volunteered (from time to time) at the art gallery and the music conservatory. She was particularly adept at fundraising, and helped organize the type of social events that were covered by both national newspapers.

Their son's decision to leave the family home at twenty-two had been a surprise. At first he lived in residence but then decided to rent a room in an ethnic neighbourhood. He told them that it would be quiet and easier for him to study there.

William had been given all the advantages a young man in this country could have. Private schools, elite summer camps, winter vacations in St. Martin's and Aruba. They expected great things from him. It was a disappointment, then, when he'd announced his interest in going into dentistry. They'd tried to redirect his interests by suggesting law or medicine, or engineering or architecture, or even accounting, but to no avail.

William's own dentist, one of the best in the city, had a large house and three ex-wives. A charming man, his female patients seemed to find him particularly attractive and his hygienists appeared to be in love with him. He was well respected in the Dental Association and travelled to Third World countries where he provided free dental work. The Wheelers privately blamed him for William's fascination with dentistry.

Geoffrey was semi-retired, having made his fortune by the age of forty-five. He now flew across the country on regular jaunts to attend meetings and golf with former associates. Julie typically accompanied him and spent time with the other wives. They had acquired friends in a number of cities—Chicago, New York, Atlanta, Seattle, San Francisco—and would plan mini-holidays with them in order to stay in touch. It was a busy life. Julie was skilful at booking time with people around Geoffrey's business commitments and so they were often able to mix business with pleasure.

Julie had the unique gift of making everyone feel, just for the moment, that they were the most important person in the room. She could focus on someone's story with genuine interest and intensity, conveying an irresistible sense that she alone could really understand them. William had fallen prey to this repeatedly in his childhood. He would open his heart to her and pour out his small troubles, and in the bliss of that moment she would comfort him. But she would neglect to ask him afterwards about those troubles and never remembered the names of his friends or teachers.

As a small child, when William was sick with a flu or cold, Julie would attempt to pamper him with things like instant chicken noodle soup or tepid tea and honey made with hot tap water. Still, the feel of Julie's hand on his brow, those rare stolen minutes with her alone in his room, always made William feel beloved, even if she had to rush off somewhere to a dinner party or a private showing.

Geoffrey, too, adored Julie. He often called her his little Barbie doll, which she took as the highest of compliments. She loved to dress up, go to the beauty salon, and walk out for the evening with her husband. She saw it as her duty to be his private showpiece and to look good for him. Managing the household and their social life was easily done. She and Geoffrey shared a part-time secretary who made all their travel arrangements and booked the caterers and florists for them. The housekeeper and gardener took care of everything else. Julie was able to concentrate on supplementing her wardrobe with a few new pieces and maintaining her trim figure by playing vigorous tennis as often as possible.

TARA

Stella slipped on an old jacket and went out to the back garden, where the leaves were already ankle deep. Raking furiously at first, she tried to instill order. The smell was fragrant and the air fresh. She found herself relaxing, and as she worked she was glad to have some time to herself to think about what her mother had said. Small piles of leaves formed.

Hey, you!

Stella looked up and saw Tara standing by the wooden fence. *C'mon and join me.*

Tara unlatched the gate and walked into the yard, kicking a few leaves as she went. *Do you have a lot of work this weekend?*

A fair bit, plus whatever needs doing around here.

Let me help. Tara commandeered the rake and briskly combined two smaller piles of leaves into a larger one. Then, grabbing Stella's hand, she pulled her forward and they both fell into the pile laughing. They lay there for a moment, still holding hands.

Do you ever feel, asked Stella, *that the world is so sad you can't bear it?*

No, but then I don't have your screwed-up family. We hate each other in a much more upfront way at my house.

CRYING

Stella did not often cry. She was too practical to be self-indulgent or emotional. When she was a child, sobbing with the fresh pain of a smashed elbow or scraped knee, her mother would shush her impatiently. Stella was made to feel that her grief was an imposition on others, that it was somehow unseemly. Her father was unknowingly complicit in this, calling her as his *brave little trooper* or his *shining star*. These endearments were precious to Stella and filled her with pride. But troopers did not cry and stars needed to shine. There was no room for her tears.

Her grandfather was the only person in her close acquaintance who cried openly. Tears often leaked out and travelled down his creased face unashamedly. This was a source of wonderment to Stella. She couldn't imagine the Wheelers crying, although she'd been told that when William and Pam were married at Trinity Chapel one bright Saturday morning, Grandmother Wheeler had been inconsolable. Apparently, she was so distraught and choked so loudly that William stopped reciting his vows and left the altar to check on her. Pam would sometimes use this story as evidence of the Wheelers' dislike, claiming that Julie's display had been a deliberate attempt to abort the wedding. At these times William would smile wryly and not contradict her.

When Grandfather Lipinski cried, it was a different matter. The sadness seemed to seep out unawares. Stella's father was usually at fault. He often probed the old man's memory, asking for war stories, sometimes even ones he'd heard before. Grandfather Lipinski would settle in, his eyes going distant as though looking far away, his voice taking on a flattened, quiet monotone. His hands, their veins raised and knobby, would rest on his knees, and his words would take them all to a far-off field or village. Stella would sit quietly with her eyes closed as her father leaned forward eagerly, as though anxious to catch every nuance. Pam and Maria would retreat to the kitchen and clatter there noisily, forming a kind of domestic background noise that was easily blocked out.

It was in this way that Stella learned everything she knew about the Second World War in Europe and what little she understood about military history. Remembrance Day was a time to close her eyes, at the eleventh hour on the eleventh day of the eleventh month, and reflect on Macjiek, her grandfather's friend. She felt virtuous then, praying for a young soldier she'd never met, the war real to her. In her mind Macjiek was forever young, handsome and trim in a smart uniform, with dark, wavy hair and strong arms. This was the sort of man Stella fantasized about. A man's man. Someone who could fix anything and laugh at the world. A man with no fears.

Whenever her grandfather spoke of his friend, he cried. It was as though all the losses and all the sadness in his life, all the terror and horrific misdeeds he'd witnessed, were associated with the death of Macjiek. He could never speak of him, or of that time, without his face becoming wet. Stella would sometimes open her eyes and watch the tears drop from his chin onto the front of his shirt, forming small sodden places of distress. At these times her mother would call him *a sentimental old fool*. William and Stella would often leap to his defence, but more often than not they'd leave her unchallenged, unwilling to compromise the trance-like state Stan's words had evoked. It was simpler to ignore her.

WILLIAM'S EXPLANATION

Stella generally kept quiet when her mother went on a rant about something. *Silence means assent* was Stella's credo, and she'd reference Thomas More when her mother raged at her for *not taking sides* or for *being so damn secretive*. This would only further irritate Pam, but she was not a little intimidated by Stella's education and the gentle check would eventually serve its purpose. The rants were typically about Stella's often absent father: he worked too late, he worked too hard, he spent too much money on his rugs—a litany of grievances rendered irrelevant once William developed his *other interests* and absented himself permanently. Stella prided herself on having appeared to remain neutral when in fact she didn't ever blame her father.

Stella understood instinctively that something was lacking in her father's engagement. She believed his emotional remove to be akin to her own, that they were alike in being observers of life rather than active participants. She hadn't imagined William would seek anything outside the safe realm he'd constructed, never mind seize it so unexpectedly. His daring was what troubled her most—that she'd misread this man who had so constantly loved her. And if she'd failed to recognize what he was capable of, then surely no other man could be trusted to provide the constancy she craved.

During one of their first post-separation dinners, William tried to explain to Stella what had transpired. They were at a little Italian restaurant adjacent to the mall. He'd taken her shopping, pacing the concourse while she picked out a new winter coat. Stella always shopped efficiently, for one thing at a time; she looked only for price point and fit. William, who'd learned not to distract her by suggesting other styles or colours, had simply handed her his bank card. Now, with her new coat folded neatly in a bag on the chair beside her, they were making their way through veal parmesan.

Stella, you need to know that this is not about you. It's something I had to do. Stella stopped chewing, wiped her fingers on a paper napkin, and watched him carefully, scrutinizing his face. *I made a mistake and I had to make it right. I can't explain it to you now, but I will someday. I'll continue to look after you and your mother. I will always be your father.*

Stella looked down at her plate and picked at her food gingerly. She was silent, waiting for more.

I didn't mean to hurt you, Stella, he offered, reaching across the table and touching the back of her hand lightly with his fingers. *Is it very awful at home right now?*

Stella nodded. She could not speak.

CONSTRUCTED HAPPINESS

William loved his drive home to Boland Mills. On this night the traffic was light for a Friday, and he navigated the streets in good time. Pulling into the driveway, he saw that the living room lights were ablaze, welcoming him. It was late but he hoped Fatima was still awake. He wanted to talk to her about the long, difficult hours he'd just spent at his practice. To look at the plateaus in her sculpted face and believe she cared about the details of his day. *To know that she wanted to know.*

He locked the car and strode to the front door. Before he even reached it she was there, smiling and beckoning him inside. She helped him take off his sports coat and then moved against his chest, wrapping her arms around his waist. He kissed her forehead and ran his hands up and down the smooth fabric of her untucked blouse. Her legs were bare. It looked as though he'd caught her undressing. She must have heard the car and rushed to the door.

How's the little guy? he asked. *Is he sleeping?*

Yes, I just checked on him. Come. Have you eaten? Tugging his arm gently, Fatima led William to the living room where she'd laid out their dinner on the coffee table. *Shall I pour us some wine?*

William settled down comfortably on the stuffed leather couch. *No wine for me. I'll just eat a little something and get to bed.*

Fatima passed him a plate that he balanced on his lap. *Tell me everything.*

He speared a piece of pepper and began recounting his day. When he'd talked himself out, she sank back on the opposite corner of the couch and stretched her legs out towards him. William put his plate down, turned to her, and picked up one of her feet in his hands. Caressing it gently, he bent down and kissed her toes. Fatima squirmed a little and lowered her own plate to the floor.

Are you not hungry?

A little, but I can wait.

She slid off the couch and knelt before him, then placed her hands on his shoulders.

William smiled at his wife and kissed the top of her head. Her hair was shiny. Stylishly cut. He loved the way it swung when she talked or moved her head. It seemed full of life and movement to him. He bent his head and kissed her face, her nose, her eyes, her lips. Small, peppery kisses. His hands unbuttoned her blouse and he slipped it down her shoulders. She sat still, watching him take pleasure. Slowly, she unhooked her lace bra and leaned close to him, pressing her breasts against his shirt. William pulled her closer. His hands slipped beneath her lace panties and he caressed her bottom, felt the small heft of each cheek in his hands. He closed his eyes and sighed. *Just to hold her like this was enough,* he thought, *enough to make it worthwhile. The pain he'd caused.*

His mouth found a nipple and he nibbled it lightly, tenderly, thoughtfully. Her hands were in his hair, smoothing it and rubbing his scalp, massaging the back of his neck. She wrapped her legs around him, pressing into him. Her tongue licked his ear, she bit his earlobe. He began to concentrate only on this: his new life, his new wife, his constructed happiness. Holding her against him, he stood and carried her to the bedroom.

This room was precious to William. It was this room he closed his eyes to imagine when the stress of work became overwhelming, when he felt frightened by his mortality, when he worried about his finances, or the future of his small son. The walls were a deep paprika red and the hardwood floor was covered with carpets from his collection. No pictures or curtains or anything else. Just the fabulous carpets and the rich red walls. They had painted the room together. He'd worked furiously, energetically, determined to finish the job so that he could set up their bed. She'd laughed, saying she'd always be willing to undress if that was the secret to making him do her bidding. *That's only part of the secret*, he wanted to say. *I will always do your bidding.*

The king-sized bed allowed him to extend his legs fully, to point his feet out in a luxurious stretch and not touch the footboard. To feel encased in a private island of touching and gentleness. To know there were edges to this bliss but that he could not feel them. He lowered Fatima down on the cover and lay down beside her.

Reaching to pull her once more close to him, William noticed that the nipple he'd suckled was now inverted. Stroking it with his finger, he tried to tease it back into shape. Fatima watched him. *Has this happened before? It's gone funny. Did I hurt you?*

No, of course not, she murmured, rubbing the offending nipple. *Maybe I'm dehydrated.*

If it stays that way, I think you should get it checked.

Fatima smiled. *You worry too much.*

TANNER

Despite William's late night, the next morning he rose early. He was thinking about Stan and Maria. *Would you like to see Grandma and Grandpa and go to the big park today?* he asked Tanner at breakfast. He looked over at Fatima, who nodded. She helped

Tanner get dressed, kissed them both goodbye, and stood in the doorway as William stowed the red tricycle in the trunk of his Mercedes.

We'll be back after lunch, he called out. She waved as they drove away. William powered on the CD in the player and Tanner began to kick his legs and sing along.

When they arrived at Indian Grove, Tanner smiled and looked out the window expectantly. William unbuckled him from the car seat, and carrying him on his hip, walked to the side door and knocked. He waited only a moment for Maria to appear.

William! she cried. *Stanislaw! A surprise! Stan, come quick, William is here.* Stan emerged behind her on the stairs. He smiled to see them and put out his arms to take the little boy. Maria and Stan kissed Tanner over and over and then carried him into the living room. Maria hurried off and came back carrying a laundry basket filled with blocks and toys. Tanner sat down on the carpet and began to play.

How are you, Stan?

Nothing so much the matter. The little one, he looks good. He's growing taller.

Your namensvetter, I thought you might like to see him.

Always. Stan smiled. *We are always happy to see him.*

Would you be up to a walk in the park this morning? I brought his tricycle. You know he loves it.

Of course, said Maria, agreeing for her husband, *and then maybe you come back and have a cup of coffee and a little strudel?*

Twenty minutes later he and Stan followed closely as Tanner peddled along the park's pathway. It was a cool day and his cheeks were soon pink with the fresh air. He held out his cold pudgy hands to his Grandpa, who blew on them and then rubbed them with the sleeve of his sweater.

We should go back, said William. *It's pretty chilly out of the sun.*

William, there is something you should do.

Yes?

You should let Stella meet your son. She will be happy to know you have such a joy in your life.

I can't do that, Stan. It would hurt her. Remind her of the divorce.

She is a woman now. Her mother and grandmother were both married at her age. You should trust her with this.

Stan, I can't do that. It's better that I keep my two families apart.

But you do not keep him from us, protested Stan. *Why is that?*

William was silent—absorbing the question, feeling challenged. He formulated several possible responses but found that he couldn't utter the words. *Because I can't bear for you not to have a namensvetter, not to know that your name will be remembered and your life honoured. I can't bear for my son not to know a man who is brave and unselfish despite the horrors he's seen. I can't bear to be apart from someone who has accepted and understood me even after I hurt his family. I can't bear to think of what I might become if I don't have you in my life.*

Another day, maybe, offered Stan. *Another day, maybe we can talk. She will love him.*

Yes, said William, patting the old man on his shoulder. *Yes, another day we will talk.*

WILLIAM'S STRUGGLE

William could not fathom talking to Stella about his new family. How could you say to your grown-up daughter that you'd left her mother because you wanted to experience unfettered joy? How could you say that an old man who knew the true value of life was your closest confidant? How could you tell her that you'd been unfaithful to her mother, that you'd allowed yourself to fall in love with someone else?

How could he look into that serious face and explain how he'd felt when he learned he would once again become a father? And how could he tell her that her grandfather had wept at the news, not for sorrow but for joy? How to explain the welcoming of new life and the celebration of birth when it cost others so much? How do you balance that equation? How much good must you do in your life to atone?

These were not questions that William felt equipped to answer. It wasn't that he'd intended to exclude Stella, to cloak his new life in mystery. He'd wanted only to shield her from the brutal truth. *I no longer loved your mother. I couldn't make myself love her. We had nothing to talk about. She became uninteresting. I share responsibility for what happened to her. I'm guilty. I can't undo what she's become. I don't like myself when I'm with her. I have failed her and I am ashamed.*

EXPLANATIONS

William was silent on the way back to the house and quiet during the visit over coffee and strudel. Maria didn't seem to notice and nor did Tanner, who sat on his grandfather's lap eating pieces of cherry strudel from Stan's fingers like a small bird. William smiled to see the trusting little body nestled in close, snuggled and safe, opening his mouth and waiting for a sweet morsel. Maria continually wiped at his lips with a paper napkin, kissing him each time she did. Neither of them could be near little Stan for very long without kissing him.

On the way home, Tanner fell asleep in his car seat. William took the long way, winding along the lakeshore. It was hard to believe that he lived in such a beautiful place.

Stella, William rehearsed out loud, *I need to tell you something. You know that I have a son. His name is Stanislaw William Wheeler. My wife calls him Tanner. I named him after your grandfather. He is his namensvetter. When your mother and I were first married, I thought we'd have a son. I promised your grandfather we'd name that son after him.*

I met Fatima, and I fell in love with her. I didn't go looking for her; I met her at a rug convention. She was beautiful and smart and easy to talk to. I allowed myself to go for coffee with her and then dinner. It was wrong of me. And then I saw her again. I consulted her about a damaged rug I'd bought. She offered to introduce me to someone who could repair it. She showed me her own collection. I acted foolishly. There is no excuse for my behaviour.

When I learned she was pregnant, I went for long walks. I didn't know what to do. I didn't call Fatima and I didn't talk to your mother. And then one day I was walking in the park and saw your grandfather feeding the ducks. He came up to me. He asked me what the matter was. And I told him.

The thing is, Stella, your grandfather stood by me. Even though I'd messed up, he stood by me. "You have been a son to me, William," he said, "and you are a kind man. You will do the honourable thing."

I didn't know what he meant at first. I assumed he meant that I should stay with you and your mother. But that wasn't it at all. He told me that true honour requires courage, and that I needed to be courageous for us all.

I came to believe that staying married to your mother meant I'd be preventing her from finding her own happiness. I knew you'd be all right. And I knew that the baby would need two parents to love him. Your grandfather helped me understand that.

William sighed, then checked to make sure he hadn't wakened Tanner. He was sleeping soundly in his car seat, his neck cricked to the side. Rosy little cheeks and cherry-stained lips. There was no way he could ever say these things to Stella.

PAM'S FANTASIES

The fantasies started when William left. She found herself saying things like *Tom Selleck would really like me in this dress.* Or *Cary Grant would know a good thing when he saw it.* Or *Richard Burton would never have left me for some carpet woman.* Pam kept up her beauty regime and continued to focus on her appearance. But it was no longer a vain attempt to attract William; it was for an imaginary admirer whose identity changed depending on her mood or the latest movie she'd watched.

Stella was at university and William was gone. There was no one else. And so Pam would carefully do her hair, apply her makeup, put on the seductive lingerie she'd bought to entice her husband. She'd wear it under her clothes all day, pretending that a fantasy lover would be coming by and that she needed to be ready for him.

Pam longed for the doorbell to ring, imagining the response she'd get and how she'd respond in turn when any one in her list of potential movie star lovers finally came for her. She would be ravaged with the passionate lovemaking that would take place all over the house.

Her fantasies did not extend beyond the sex. Her entire experience with men had been limited to her adolescent encounters with one boy in the park and with William. Outside of the bedroom, she hadn't really known how to please him. His work was uninteresting to her, as were his damn carpets. Sex was her big drawing card.

THE BOOK

William carried his son into the house and laid him down in his big boy bed, making sure the pillows were lined up on the floor in case he rolled out in his sleep. Then he went to find Fatima.

She was at her desk in her little office, hunched over one of her manuscripts. By now she'd published so many papers on the rugs of Iran that she'd decided to write a book. At first she'd focused on tribal rugs, but a number of colleagues and friends had thought that too narrow, so she'd expanded it to include Kurdish rugs from Turkey, the former Soviet Union, and Syria. There were so many regional differences in the patterns and techniques that she'd written an entire section just on the primitive looms and dyes used by nomadic peoples. Although the photography would be expensive, she was determined to do the whole thing up like a coffee table art book. And she was already looking ahead: her second manuscript would be a *Decorating Guide,* with Persian carpets as the focal pieces. William was enthusiastic about both projects and always happy to see her absorbed in the work.

He told her about their morning, how happy Stan and Maria had been to see Tanner.

Oh, I'm glad. She gestured at her laptop. *I started my Introduction. I can't wait to show it to Parisa—she really wanted me to stop fiddling with the edits and try to pull it all together with this piece. Anyway, I think I'm on the right track.*

William stood and kissed his wife on the top of her head. *Keep writing. I'll check on Tanner.*

I love you.

William peeked in at his sleeping son and then went downstairs to survey the contents of the fridge. Alone in her office, Fatima continued to peck away at her laptop. It was hard to concentrate, though. She hadn't yet told William about her doctor's appointment. She'd wait for the mammogram results before she said anything.

FATIMA AND PARISA

Parisa wasn't just Fatima's cousin; she was her best friend and business partner, too. She'd agreed to locate the samples for Fatima's book and to arrange for the photography. Many of their regular customers had already agreed to have pieces from their collections included. Parisa felt that the books would be good for their business and had been urging Fatima to complete it. Finding a publisher would come later, once all the colour photographs had been assembled.

Both of their families were from Tehran. They'd left Iran together in 1979, just after the deposition of the Shah. The two cousins hadn't been close, but since arriving in Toronto they'd become inseparable.

The Kamalis, family friends who'd arrived several years earlier, had met them at the airport and helped establish them in a hotel while their documents were verified and their papers processed. The Kamalis were jewellers, and had managed to export much of their wealth and business assets before the fall of the Shah. As a young man Mr. Kamali had studied business at the University of Toronto, and that, along with his excellent English, had facilitated an easy transition for the Kamali family. Mr. Kamali took great pride in having predicted the revolution and the ensuing political and religious repression. He was an excellent host to the newly arrived families and guided them carefully through their immigration procedure. The Kamalis were well connected. They opened their home to friends and family alike, making sure the newcomers felt supported and cared for.

The Yadgars and Surins were hotel bound for three weeks, and it was during this time that Parisa and Fatima discovered how much they had in common. Both girls loved Western music and happily spent hours with Jannat Kamali, who now called herself Jan, learning the steps to the Village People's "YMCA." *Happy Days* was a particular favourite; on weeknights both families would sit in front of the black-and-white TV watching the North Americans solve their difficulties and laughing at Fonzie's thumbs-up. Mr. Surin believed that English television was an excellent way to improve their language skills.

Acting on Mr. Kamali's advice, Mr. Yadgar and Mr. Surin had pooled their finances and hired an immigration lawyer to process their paperwork. This expedited the red tape and they were cleared fairly quickly.

NEWCOMERS

The families rented a large townhouse together, sharing everything while they became established. Parisa's father, who'd worked as an accountant in the oil industry in Tehran, was able to find employment at Petro-Canada. It was an entry-level clerk's position, but his accounting and his English skills were good and he was soon promoted. Fatima's father, who'd been a senior professor of political science at the University of Tehran, initially took a job at a local convenience store. Eventually, though, he was able to secure sessional work at York University, and began anew the task of establishing himself in a tenure track. His firsthand accounts of Islamic regime change, his lectures, and his published papers were all well received by the academic community.

Despite the setback in status these jobs entailed, the men were delighted to have found work in their areas. Mrs. Yagdar and Mrs. Surin were sisters, and both were enchanted with their new home and shared household. They cooked and shopped together, clinging to each other with locked arms as they navigated the unfamiliar suburban streets and grocery stores.

Fatima and Parisa were placed in the same classes at high school, ate lunch together, and walked back and forth to school side by side. Their school had many newcomers, and the girls were not alone in needing to improve their language skills and trying to understand the social expectations. The girls had attended segregated schools in Tehran and felt uncomfortable sitting next to boys and brushing against them in the packed hallways.

Both girls suffered the ignominy of never quite fitting in. Although they were Persian refugees, they were not, as most people assumed, Muslims. Their families were Jewish, and still observed their faith traditions. Their more secular friends and classmates didn't understand why they couldn't go to the movies or a dance on Friday night. This small anomaly created a barrier to their social acceptability. Their Temple was orthodox; opportunities for mixing with boys outside of school were restricted and closely monitored. As a result, despite their fathers' liberal ideology, the girls suffered a sense of alienation that drew them even more closely together.

FATIMA'S STORY

Fatima was fifteen when the Shah was overthrown. Her father hoped the regime change was temporary, but when some of his academic colleagues disappeared he worried for his own safety and that of his family. His only child, Fatima, attended a French international school for girls. When it was shut down Professor Surin registered her at a neighbourhood school, where the boys and girls were kept apart and the curriculum taught in the context of Islam. He still believed this to be a short-lived interruption in their lives. Meanwhile, girls and women were now required to cover themselves when in public. No signs of vanity or beauty were permitted.

Once a week the students at Fatima's school were taken on a ski trip to the mountains. The boys sat at the front of the bus and the girls at the back, their teachers making sure they didn't speak to one another. And once they were outside on the slopes, the teachers kept them separated. Fatima loved to ski—the feeling of freedom as she sped down the hill, the crisp winter air stinging her face. She felt alive and filled with energy and joy as she concentrated on her movements, at one with the mountain and her skis.

At the bottom of a run one day, Fatima and two other girls were arrested. They hadn't kept their knees covered, and one had lost her headscarf in the wind. Prevented from calling their parents, they were taken to jail. For three days they were held in a filthy cell, interrogated about their parents and their neighbours and tested on their understanding of Islam. On the third day they were released and permitted to call home.

Professor Surin had been distraught when the bus returned without his daughter. The staff wouldn't speak to him, pushing past him as though he were invisible. He didn't know whether Fatima had been hurt or arrested or had simply missed the bus. He drove to the ski resort and tried to ask questions but no one would tell him anything. He didn't know that two other girls were also missing. He feared going home to his wife without his daughter. He couldn't imagine her grief, her questions, their shared terror. He sat in his car and cried.

At home, his wife was at prayer. She knew something was wrong. The bus always returned late from the mountains, her husband always there to meet it. But it was many hours past their usual arrival time. Fatima should come rushing inside, hungry from her exercise, smelling of the outdoors and wind, her father carrying his heavy briefcase filled with student papers to be marked late into the night. They should sit together and have their meal, and she would give thanks that for one more week they were all safe. But they did not come.

By the time the phone rang three days later with instructions to pick up their daughter, the Surins were dazed with terror and grief. Professor Surin drove to get Fatima while her mother continued to wring her hands and keen. Neither knew what had befallen her or why. The not knowing blocked any sense of relief or thanksgiving.

Fatima was catatonic when her father collected her from the police. He scanned her quickly and took her into his arms. He spoke to no one as he guided her to the waiting car. She had no visible bruises, but he understood that violence left deeper marks that could not be seen and could not be healed.

The following morning he called in sick and spent the day consulting privately about arrangements for he and his family to visit a colleague in France. Surreptitiously, he liquidated as many assets as he could without attracting notice. They left some valuables with family and friends and sewed money and jewellery into the lining of his heavy tweed jacket. Their trip to France was effortless. He showed the officials a paper he'd written, "The Benefits of Islamic Regime Change," which he said he'd be presenting at a conference in France. The officials did not ask for conference details, nor did they check the contents of the paper. If they had, they would have seen that the title page was a recent addition to an older paper he'd written about something else entirely.

In France, the Surins waited for the Yagdars to join them, and together the two families prepared to emigrate to Canada, whose point system readily facilitated the entry of those with their education and professional credentials. Fatima did not recover her ability to speak for several weeks. She had terrible nightmares and couldn't go to sleep unless her mother was beside her, holding her close. When Parisa joined them in France, Fatima clung to her cousin. Slowly, for the first time since her ordeal, she began to relax.

PARISA

A year after they finished high school, Parisa married a man from their Temple. He was a carpet merchant who wanted an intelligent wife to help him with his business, one who could speak, read, and write both English and Farsi. He wasn't looking for a woman to breed sons or be a traditional wife, but he wanted the comfort of someone who shared his cultural experiences and took an avid interest in his work.

Parisa wasn't repulsed by Parvez, and was keenly interested in making money. He drove a good car, had a respectable store on Wellington Street, and seemed in all things to be gentle, kind, and reasonable. She went out with him several times before deciding to marry him.

She quickly learned the business, becoming a proficient saleswoman. She began to dress in expensive, form-fitting black dresses and spiky heels and wore large amounts of gold jewellery. Her fragrance was musky with a hint of sweetness to it, and she'd sometimes spray a bit of it in the showroom before meeting a client.

Parisa's attractive presence soon necessitated the hire of a second assistant, and that's when Fatima found employment. She enjoyed working with her cousin and slid easily into the routines Parisa and her husband had established. She became deeply interested in the rugs they were importing and selling and began to accompany them on buying trips. Eventually, their roles shifted slightly. Parvez would stand back while Fatima did the selecting, and then, signals exchanged, he would negotiate the pricing and complete the transaction. The threesome formed a close, and successful, partnership.

UNWELCOME NEWS

Parisa didn't like William. She liked his money and she liked his penchant for collecting their rugs, but she didn't like *him*. She didn't trust a man who was married to one woman and dated another. What's more, Parvez didn't like him either. He was furious when Fatima announced, over coffee one morning, that she was pregnant.

Pfaw. Parvez turned away from her. *I curse the dog who shamed you.*

I am not shamed, Fatima shot back. *I'm carrying a baby but I am not shamed.*

You have shamed all of us. You are family. This will hurt our business.

Why? Why should it have to? Why is this anyone's concern but mine?

It is our concern, you fool. Parvez was raising his voice now. *You can't travel, you can't be seen in public, you'll become restricted. And then, when the baby comes, there'll be more trouble. Crying and babysitters and sickness. How could you be so stupid?*

Protectively, instinctively, Fatima placed her hand across the not yet discernible baby mound. She glared at him. *Do you want me to quit? Are you better off without me? Is that what you want?*

Please, interjected Parisa. *We need a plan, that's all. Let's just think for a minute and make a plan.*

There is no plan, said Parvez. *This William comes and is allowed to take what he wants, and you both let him, and now we're ruined. Everything we've worked for is ruined. How can a plan fix that?*

How can you blame me for this? Parisa objected. *I had nothing to do with it.*

You? You had everything to do with it. You allowed her to see this man alone, and now, now you see what has happened? The blame is yours also.

Stop it! Both of you, Fatima shouted. *Just stop it. I'll work in the back, away from the customers. I'll find ways to expand the business using the computer and the telephone. No one will have to see me. We'll go on a big buying trip before I begin to show, and we'll increase our inventory to last for a year. After that, we can make arrangements for the baby.*

Parvez left the warehouse and didn't return for the rest of the day. Parisa sat in the back room and fidgeted. Fatima stood up slowly, smoothed the fabric of her dress, and walked to the office to begin working. It was soon after this that she began writing essays on Iranian rugs and having them published. She loved the research, she loved the writing, but she also reasoned that more people would want to own Persian carpets if they understood their history and their value. That was her plan.

THE PROPOSAL

William's proposal of marriage surprised her. She'd had no expectations. She hadn't thought about their relationship in any sort of permanent way. The ring he gave her was a square-cut, full-carat diamond. He said he was *invested*. This little play on words amused her: he invested in rugs, he invested in large diamond rings, he was invested in her and in the future of their child. This word became her secret mantra. *Invested. He was invested in her.*

An Unpleasant Visit

Stella had spent the day running errands for her mother and thought it would be nice to drop by her grandparents' place. Pam agreed to come as long as Stella did the driving and promised not to stay too late. On the way they picked up a freshly baked apple pie. Pam sat in the car and waited for Stella while she ran in. She was in a relatively good mood.

Luby, Pamela, come in, greeted her grandmother. *Stan, Stan, come quick, the girls are here.* Maria kissed Stella and Pam as they walked inside and passed her the pie. Stan turned off the television and came into the kitchen to join them.

A nice surprise, he said, *and a pie also. We should have a coffee.*

Stella walked over to her grandfather and went to kiss him. He smiled at her, but then suddenly his face changed. *Stella, what is this you are wearing?* He pointed at her blazer. She'd recently polished the antique edelweiss pins and sewn them onto her lapel.

Aren't they pretty? I found them in an antique store.

You don't know what you are doing! At this, Stan picked up the boxed pie from the table and threw it in the sink. *Take it off! I do not want this Nazi shit in my house.*

Stella was shocked and did not know what to say. His face had transformed and his eyes were flashing. This wasn't something she'd ever witnessed before; it seemed utterly out of character. It didn't make sense.

Pamela stood up and faced her father. *What are you talking about?*

Take it off! He was red-faced and crying now. Maria was cowering in the corner.

Grandpa, what have I done? What's wrong?

That's Nazi bullshit you are wearing.

Stella was trembling. She took off her jacket and looked at the brooches. *Is it these?*

He grabbed the jacket from her and threw it on the floor. He spit on it and then crushed it with his foot. He swore in Polish, a long litany of something Stella did not understand.

Pa, calm down. She didn't know. She didn't mean anything. She took it off, Pa. Relax. Pam reached out to pat his shoulder, but he pushed her arm away.

It's no make a difference! Stan stormed from the kitchen and left the house. They heard the door bang.

Grandma, I'm sorry, I didn't know. I just thought they were pretty.

WILLIAM'S FIRST ENGAGEMENT

William's parents were distraught when he came home one weekend and broke the news of his engagement over drinks on the patio. Julie, who was nursing a sherry at the time, let out a gasp and in doing so dropped her crystal glass on the flagstone, where it smashed into tiny shards.

Geoffrey couldn't get his son to hear reason. William's sense of honour was infuriating. It was clear that this girl was taking advantage of him, that her parents were taking advantage of him, that he was being entirely naive.

Under duress, Geoffrey and Julie agreed to meet the girl for dinner at the club the following evening. William had already called to make a reservation. He wouldn't stay the night, insisting he had to get back to the city. His parents were convinced that *the Polack* was manipulating him and that he needed some distance from her in order to make some sensible decisions.

Julie dressed carefully for the club, choosing her favourite salmon-coloured wool crepe ensemble with the tiny mink collar and cuffs. Geoffrey had on a navy blue pin-striped suit. They resolved to be gracious, for appearances' sake, and to follow up throughout the week with a series of arguments meant to elicit William's better judgment.

In the interim, just to be safe, Geoffrey called a friend at his bank, and another at his law firm, to see whether he could protect William's trust fund from an unsavoury alliance.

DINNER AT THE CLUB

Pam was nervous when she went downstairs to meet William. She had curled her hair and it was springing around her shoulders in black glossy spirals. And she was wearing a dress he'd never seen before: dusty rose with a high collar, lots of tucks and pleats in the skirt, a matching bow tied around her waist. She looked like a parcel about to be unwrapped. He couldn't wait to be alone with her in the car. She was twisting her engagement ring, a single solitaire diamond.

Stan and Maria stood warily at the bottom of the stairs watching them leave. William waved at them cheerfully. Pam looked over her shoulder and said something in Polish. She sounded frightened.

It'll be fine, William assured her. *They're nice people. You have nothing to worry about.*

Pamela knew differently. She sensed that William's people would find her wanting in some way, or that they'd guess she was pregnant. She felt stupid and uneducated. She'd been dreading this dinner, even though she knew it was necessary and part of the course she had chosen for herself.

The drive took almost an hour. William kept stealing glances at Pam, who was fidgeting with her bow, wrapping it around her fingers and then pulling it out into a long spiral. Her apprehension contributed to his own, and by the time they arrived at the club William was filled with a sense of foreboding.

His parents were sitting in the lounge, where low-slung chairs facing the golf course were scattered throughout its expanse. William spotted them in a far corner, away from the other guests, staring out at the green and not speaking. They stood for the introductions. His father was marginally warmer than his mother, but Julie, apparently unable to help herself, scanned Pamela's dress and hair critically before shaking hands. William saw the distaste flash across her face before she assumed her polite smile.

The four of them moved to the dining room. Geoffrey and Julie floated through the crowd greeting friends. William exchanged a few remarks with some of his own. When he introduced Pamela she'd smile coyly and look down. After they were seated at their usual table Julie began listing the people she knew in the room—her way of establishing that there were those who belonged at the club and those who did not.

Mother was all William said, but she knew what he meant.

So there's going to be a wedding, Geoffrey began, looking at Pamela. *Have you set a date yet?*

I thought I would let William decide.

A long engagement would be a good thing, Julie chimed in. *It will give us time to do things right.*

No, said William. *I want it sooner rather than later. Something small and intimate.*

Well, surely Pamela has a say, said Julie. *I'm sure you'd like a big fancy wedding, wouldn't you, dear?*

I like small. A small wedding would be fine.

But there are so many people to include. Invitations to reciprocate. We've been to so many of our friends' children's weddings, and we have to ask them in turn.

Mother, I'm sorry. William looked at her sternly while reaching for Pam's hand. Trying to steady her.

Yes of course, said Geoffrey, *whatever you say. Have you thought about a location? Here at the club perhaps?*

No, I don't think so. Maybe the university. I have to call them and see if I can book a chapel.

A chapel?

Yes, a chapel. Maybe Hart House. I'll see what I can get.

I've never been there, said Pam.

You'll like it, dear, said Julie. *It's very intimate, with striking windows. You would know it if you'd ever been a student at the university.*

Mother, William cautioned once more.

Making Things Work

Fatima knew that William wrestled with his guilt and grief over leaving his wife and daughter. He wouldn't skimp on his commitment to Stella or to Pamela's maintenance, and although his lawyer and his accountant counselled moderation, he instead worked longer hours at his practice.

Fatima encouraged him to continue his visits to the Lipinskis. She knew how much the older gentleman in particular meant to him.

The Wheelers, unsurprisingly, didn't offer to meet Fatima. His father's advice had only to do with prenuptial agreements and pension splitting. William seemed depressed whenever he spoke with them. Fatima's own parents were cool with William. They viewed him as an intruder who had violated their daughter and brought dishonour to their family. He wasn't Jewish. He didn't even profess to be much of a Christian. Professor Surin had difficulty with people who had undefined ideologies and faith practices. It was for him a matter of deep principle.

And so Fatima and William retreated quietly to their own house to spend time together decorating and landscaping and cooking. Fatima would sometimes talk about her home in Tehran. She found the Canadian winters damp and missed the constant presence of a warm, bright sun and the fragrance of orange blossoms. She told him about how frequent the visitors had been, the impromptu gifts of dates and fruit and baking they would bring. She spoke fondly of all the extra guests at the dinner table, the sounds of laughter and music.

Fatima's Dreams

Fatima often had vivid dreams and nightmares, and would describe these to William when they woke in the early morning. He'd stroke her gently as she recounted the panic of her nighttime terror. One repeated dream had Fatima's family about to flee Tehran. Their house was partly emptied, their belongings in suitcases. They had said their goodbyes and were preparing to leave for the airport. But when Fatima went to her room to get dressed she couldn't find her clothes. She had nothing to wear. Her family was waiting but she was trapped in her room, ashamed to appear before them naked and frightened they'd leave without her.

Another recurring dream was of her grandmother dancing a traditional dance at a family gathering in Tehran. She reached for Fatima and beckoned her to join in. Fatima grasped her hand and began to mimic her grandmother's measured steps and graceful hand gestures. Suddenly, someone threw a black cloth over Fatima's head and she couldn't see. But she continued to dance to the music, slowly undulating as she'd seen her grandmother do and gradually realizing that everyone had left and she was dancing alone.

William didn't quite know what these dreams signified for Fatima, but he soothed her with the same words he used to soothe Stella when she was a child wakened by bad dreams: *Everything will be all right . . . I'm here now . . . I'll look after you.* Gentle words and small acts of kindness were his only artillery against such trauma.

Fatima began to teach William a few phrases in Farsi. He found the pronunciation difficult and the awkward sounds he made unpleasant, but he was proud of his small lexicon. He hoped with some key phrases to one day impress Parisa and Parvez. He knew they distrusted him. He felt judged by them, and by all of Fatima's family, and hoped to someday convince them of his devotion.

SHOCK

Stella was still shaken by her grandfather's reaction to the brooches. Pam, for her part, had raged against him most of the way home to Waldham. Stella had almost cried but the tears wouldn't come, and now she was craving time alone to absorb it all. After Stan had stormed out she'd stood in the kitchen watching her mother and grandmother clean up the pie, asking herself what had just happened.

I've never seen him mad before, Mom.

Well, it happens, Stella. People aren't perfect. I've seen him mad lots of times.

But he threw the pie. And he actually spit on my jacket!

Luby, Maria said, *Stan loves you and he will be sorry for making you upset. Anything to do with that terrible time upsets him.* She walked over to Stella and put her arms around her, squeezing her in a deep hug. *He will be so sorry, luby.*

Pam retrieved Stella's jacket and balled it up tightly. *This is old anyway, Stella, let's just replace it.* She stuffed the jacket and its offending brooches into the kitchen garbage.

TEACHING

Stella didn't choose teaching; she just ended up back where she started. Teachers' college seemed the logical step after her B.A. Everyone had told her she was smart and that she'd be good at it. Her father was proud when she got in. Her mother, pleased. She practice-taught in Waldham and in Elgin, in Grey Stone and in Sentinel. Familiar places, familiar family names, familiar expectations. It was relatively easy to please people, to move behind the desk at the front of the classroom and orchestrate the day. She earned glowing teaching reports. And then Old Murphy retired, and suddenly Waldham had an opening. The principal and staff remembered her as an excellent student, and even though her interview was stiff and uncomfortable, they hired her. She was, after all, one of their own. Her father was ecstatic. Her mother was just relieved she had a job.

But Stella felt trapped by the familiar. She didn't want to think *this is all there was*. You leave home, go to university, and then move back home. What kind of life trick was that?

Grandmother Lipinski suggested that Stella take a break. That she do some travelling first. As a graduation present, she and Stan gave her a brown Samsonite suitcase and an envelope containing $3500. *You should have a holiday*, her grandfather said, pressing the envelope into her hands. *You worked hard and now you should celebrate. You are the first in our family to graduate from university.*

Stella was overwhelmed by the present. She put it in the bank and thought about it guiltily. She wondered if they could afford it. She wondered if she should tell her mother about it. Finally she mentioned it to her father, who laughed at her reluctance to spend the money. *It's a gift, Stella, and you'll hurt their feelings if you don't use it.*

And so, reassured, she confided in Tara, who always knew what to do. Tara suggested they plan a holiday for the following summer.

Stella made an appointment to meet her new department head during the last week of August. She dressed smartly in a cotton khaki skirt, white blouse, and new sandals and tucked a spiral-bound notebook and a couple of pens in her bag so that she could scribble down anything important. Arlene Thacker, hired since Stella had graduated, was a scary witch of a woman. She had long, unkempt greying hair and bottle-thick glasses and wore thick black leotards, Birkenstocks, and a loose-fitting corduroy sack. Stella found herself wondering why she'd worried about making a good impression. Arlene gave her a copy of her timetable, pointed vaguely at the book room, and told Stella she could help herself to anything she wanted. She also gestured towards a shelf filled with binders. These, apparently, held the course outlines, and Stella was to access them as well. Then Arlene led her to a grime-covered desk in the corner of a narrow basement office and said that Stella should make herself at home. Her obligations fulfilled, Arlene picked up her filthy coffee mug and wandered off.

Stella stood in the empty room wondering if she was dismissed or expected to wait upon Arlene's return. After a while she returned to the school office, flipped through the binders, studied the course outlines, and chose the ones she'd need for the following week. She was grateful for the friendlier secretaries, who showed her how to make photocopies and gave her a small mountain of forms to complete. Stella slipped away in the early afternoon and drove along country roads, trying not to cry.

Stella's desk was in the Cadaver Room, which was just the right size for a hospital gurney with one cadaver. Human dissection had once been done here by grade thirteen students, who weren't allowed to actually touch the body but stood in two facing rows while their teacher flipped back the leathered skin to expose muscle groups and organs. When Stella was a student, the principal put an end to the practice and had the corpse picked up by someone from the hospital.

Older, squeamish staff still refused to enter the room, but Stella had no such qualms and found herself enjoying its quiet privacy. Another advantage was its long black Bakelite counters and many cupboards. Stella delighted in the organizational luxury this gave her and spaced her belongings neatly around the room. By way of decoration, she arranged a stuffed beaver in a tableau near the door. It would be her welcoming committee, of sorts.

Stella often heard a critical voice in her head that sounded increasingly like that of her mother. At a staff get-together after school: *You might as well go home, Stella. It's clear nobody here wants to spend time with you.* When trying on a new outfit in the store: *There's no point spending all this money. You still look plain as a dishrag.* When going out with Tara: *I don't know what you girls are after. Men want only one thing and when they're done with you, there's nothing left.* Stella believed that positive self-talk was the only way she could stop the nagging voice, so she'd written herself little messages on index cards and had affixed these to the inside of the medicine cabinet. She studied them in the morning when brushing her teeth. They filled her with the confidence she needed to go downstairs, encounter her mother, and face the day.

> *Death and sorrow will be the companions of our journey; hardship our garment; constancy and valour our only shield. We must be united, we must be undaunted, we must be inflexible.* ~ Churchill

Roses have thorns, and silver fountains mud; Clouds and eclipses stain both moon and sun. ~ Shakespeare

I celebrate myself and sing myself, And what I assume you shall assume. ~ Whitman

We are not interested in the possibilities of defeat. ~ Queen Victoria

Laid flat under the clear plastic of her desk blotter was a collection of old Valentines she'd carefully saved. *You will always be my little star,* from her father. *Beloved* from her grandparents. *Best friend* from Tara. The cards themselves were old but they were Stella's touchstones. Words that verified she mattered.

SAND

Stella felt hesitant about visiting her grandparents after the pie incident. Pamela noticed she hadn't been for a couple of weeks and probed her gently at breakfast.

People aren't perfect, Stella. You know they're crazy proud of you. They'll be hurt if you stay away too long.

I'm not staying away, I'm just busy.

Busy, schmizzy. You're avoiding them.

I've never seen Grandpa that upset before.

Stella, look, if you don't go, I'll have to. And I don't like the long drive on the Parkway. All those cars give me a headache and I get anxious. Do you want to make me go?

No, Mom, I can go. I just don't know when.

It'll be fine. They'll be happy to see you. Your grandfather will act like nothing ever happened. Trust me.

How do you know?

I lived with him long enough, that's how I know. If you even bring it up, he'll say something like "Sand over it now."

Sand over it now?

He has this crazy theory. He says that the waves wash away every-thing on the beach, and that means you start every new day fresh. You don't revisit upsets or fights. You just get on with it.

But that's not how he feels about the Nazis.

No. True. But that's how he feels about family. You start fresh and get on with it. Now stop putting it off and go see them.

PINOCCHIO

Stella was often lonely. There were men on staff who would happily buy her a beer on a Friday night. There were women on staff who would easily include her in their lunches and trips to the mall. She knew this. She knew it was *something in her* that kept her aloof and frightened. Students sometimes asked her to supervise a dance or help out with a club. She would agree, ten-tatively, but then find it necessary to fabricate an excuse. Intimacy often seemed overwhelming.

One Friday night, Stella found herself driving to Toronto. As a pretext for missing a school social that evening, she'd told her department head that she had an engagement there. She couldn't afford to be seen in Waldham, and so made herself go to the city to spend the evening alone. She drove to the Beaches and found a side street to park her car. Walking along Queen Street, she window-shopped at leisure.

The vivid colours of a toy store caught her attention. Oversized giraffes were grazing in the front window. A miniature fire truck and Jaguar were parked outside the door, carefully chained to a steel post. Stella walked inside. The bright yellow lighting was intense and she blinked as she became accustomed to the glare. The place seemed chaotic. Loud children's music of some type was playing. Balloons and stuffed animals dangled from the ceiling. There were no clear sightlines and no defined aisles to walk along. She stepped carefully to the right, past bins of beach balls and bubble-blower. Moving forward slowly, she turned her head, looking for a display of children's books or teaching materials. She walked past play centres with blocks, past a section of baby toys, past a whole wall of games. She strolled on through the store, amazed at the proliferation of offerings.

Gauze-like material in shimmering pink, purple, and blue was suspended from a nearby corner. Stella moved towards it. As she drew near, she saw that little figures were hanging from the ceiling, swaying slightly amid the coloured gauze. Intrigued, she quickened her step and found herself standing beneath a gossamer tent filled with marionettes. It was mesmerizing. Goats from *The Sound of Music* were suspended overhead. She touched them and saw that their legs were jointed, allowing for movement and dance. Along with Disney characters—Mickey Mouse, Donald Duck, Goofy—were princesses, all of them beautifully painted, with exquisite detailed costumes and carefully arranged hair.

Stella was enchanted. She stood below the cloud of tiny figures and tapped them gently, urging them to dance for her. They seemed full of life and vitality. And then she saw Pinocchio. He was brightly painted in primary colours and had a little leather hat and leather shorts. But the clever thing was that his nose was a removable dowel. In a tiny plastic bag stapled to his shorts was a second nose, a longer nose. The nose that grew when he told lies. It could be twisted in when the short stub nose was taken out. Stella took it down from the hook instinctively, without thinking. Holding the wooden crosspiece in her hand, she read the cardboard tag: this marionette had been hand-crafted in Quebec with hand-stitched clothing. Pinocchio could be hers for the princely sum of one hundred and thirty-nine dollars and ninety-nine cents. It was a ridiculous amount of money for a toy. But it was Pinocchio, and he was smiling at her.

She walked to the front and found a clerk dressed in red overalls. She handed over her Visa card. Minutes later, bright yellow bag with blue tissue in hand, she left the store carrying her new love. This wasn't the sort of thing Stella typically did. She'd buy herself clothes and shoes for work, but mostly she saved her money, and never spent impulsively. Placing the bag on the front seat of her car, she tried to rationalize what she'd done.

It was only seven o'clock; she still had a couple of hours to fill before she could return to Waldham. Driving cautiously, she headed downtown. Queen Street was congested, so she swerved onto Woodbine and headed towards the Gardiner Expressway, where she sped across the city and got off at Jameson Avenue in the west end. She'd already decided to heed Pamela's advice and finally visit her grandparents. Stella turned onto their street and slowed down. She hesitated when she saw her father's Mercedes in the driveway—something might be wrong. She pulled in behind him, then hurried to the door and knocked sharply.

THE SURPRISE VISIT

Her grandmother opened the door. *Stella, luby, come in! Your father is here.* Kissing her on the forehead, Stella moved inside, dropped her purse at the landing, and walked into the kitchen, where William and Stan were sitting at the table. Playing with blocks on the floor by their feet was a small boy, dressed beautifully in dark overalls with little running shoes. He looked at her and smiled. William stood up awkwardly to greet her, glancing down at the boy apprehensively.

Stella, it's so good to see you. He hesitated. *This is my son, Stan. His mother calls him Tanner.* Her father had coloured red, the top of his ears a brilliant scarlet. He leaned towards her and pecked her cheek.

Stan beamed at her. *Sit,* he beckoned, *we are going to have cake. It's coming somebody's birthday.*

Stella flopped into a kitchen chair and stared at her father. Then she looked at her grandparents, who were watching her cautiously. Finally she looked down at the little boy. He was clearly lovely. *This is a surprise,* she finally said.

Yes, William agreed. *Not how I would have planned it.*

Maybe I should just go.

No! barked her grandfather. *You are family. This is a birthday party.*

Tanner looked up at this. He moved towards his grandfather, inserting himself between his thin knees and reclining there comfortably as he gazed at Stella.

Hello, Tanner, she offered. *How are you?*

Stan pulled him up into his lap. *This is Stella*, he said. *She is your big sister.*

Tanner stared at her and inserted a finger in his mouth.

Stella looked at William. *Where's his mother?*

At home. We're having a small party tomorrow. She's getting the house ready.

Come, said Stan, *I think there is a present somewhere.* He walked Tanner to the living room, Stella and William following. A bulky package wrapped in shiny gold paper sat waiting on the coffee table. Together, the old man and the small boy tore at the paper and unveiled a very large brown teddy bear.

This is Wojtek, said Stan. *He is a very brave bear.*

Stella watched her father's face. He kept looking at Tanner and Stan with quick, darting glances. But he wouldn't look at Stella. She was confused. She'd wanted to meet the boy for a long time, to be a part of her father's new life. But to see him here had taken her aback. How often did they visit? Was it only she and her mother who were excluded from this intimacy? What did it mean?

Tanner hugged the bear and carried it to his father. *Wojtek will protect you*, said William. *He is a very clever bear.* Stella knew the story. She'd often heard about the real Polish bear who'd served in the war—carrying ammunition, eating lit cigarettes, drinking vodka and beer. At the end of the war he'd been taken to the Edinburgh Zoo, where he lived to an old age.

And now for cake, said Maria.

When William switched off the light Stella felt an immediate release of pressure in the dimness. She knew what was coming, the cake and the sparklers and the singing, but for the moment she sank into the dark, the calm. She put her hands to her cheeks; they were warm and feverish. Her grandparents would be upset if she left. They wouldn't understand it. This was her chance to shine. To be an adult and to embrace the unexpected. She willed herself to stay, to sing the happy birthday song, to enter in.

And the boy was beautiful. She openly assessed his features, his colouring, his pudgy fingers and dark eyes. He looked loved.

He looked at home. He looked confident. It was she who needed the bear, thought Stella. She who needed a soldier to protect her and give her courage.

Maria came in carrying a birthday cake with sparklers on the glass plate reserved for such occasions.

Ooooh. Tanner grinned at the sparkling lights, clapping his little hands together. *Oooooh.*

Make a wish and blow, encouraged Maria, puckering her lips to demonstrate.

Make a wish.

Together William and Tanner blew, but when the sparklers went out little Stan looked startled and began to cry. *Awl gone.*

Stella laughed. Her grandfather laughed. Maria rushed out as William tried to comfort Tanner. *It's supposed to happen,* he said. *That's how we make a wish.*

Awl gone, howled Tanner.

Maria returned with a box of matches and relit the sparklers. Tanner stopped crying and clapped his hands. They all gazed at the sparklers. No one said anything. Tanner watched the lights on his birthday cake fizzle and spark until they burned down to short little stumps and stopped flickering altogether. Then he turned his face to his father's chest and burrowed in.

I think he's tired, it's past his bedtime.

The four adults sat quietly in the darkened living room until it was obvious that the boy had fallen asleep in his father's embrace. William carried him upstairs, returning a few minutes later.

He'll be fine for now, he said. *Let's have some cake.*

In the kitchen Grandmother Lipinski cut generous slabs and scooped a large dollop of ice cream on top of each piece. She busied herself at the stove, readying the old-fashioned percolator for a strong pot of coffee. Stella continued to steal glances at her father. He looked the same. And yet something had happened. She was here. He was here. And there was a boy sleeping upstairs. A small, beautiful boy with a soldier bear. Her brother.

Well, Stella, William began, *what have you been up to?*

Stella felt challenged. Defensive. *Not much. I was shopping, out for a drive, thought I'd stop by.*

William attacked his cake with the fork. *How's school?*

About the same. I'm teaching Romeo and Juliet.

Ah, the love story? interjected her grandfather.

You could call it that, Stella said, *or you could call it a tragedy, since they both die.*

To die for love, said Stan, *is not so bad.*

It was unnecessary. And just dumb. Stella heard the heat in her own voice and was surprised by it. She didn't really feel that way about the young lovers. She envied them. To burn with such passion was surely worth an early death. To just that once experience feelings so intense, so honest and so real. She couldn't say that, though; they would think her sentimental, and this was not in her nature.

A true love story, Stan remarked, *is a rare and wonderful thing.*

I should go, Stella said abruptly. *It's getting late.*

Wait awhile, Stella, her father said gently. *It's not that late. Have a visit first.*

No. I should really go. She carried her plate to the sink and tried to compose herself. It was too much, really. Her father looked awkward. *He looks like a nice boy, Dad,* she offered. *I was glad to meet him.* It was the most she had. All that she could offer.

She kissed Maria on the cheek. *See you soon, Grandma.* Then she crossed the kitchen to her grandfather.

He stood up and hugged her. *You did good,* he said quietly. Stella smiled.

I'll walk you out, William offered.

Stella left the house quickly, inhaling a deep breath of air as she walked to her car. William crossed the driveway behind her and she braced herself. She was tired and didn't want a confrontation. Emotional experiences always drained her. He started to speak, she saw his mouth forming words, but she shook her head and held up her hand.

Dad, I have something for Tanner. Please give it to him on his birthday. She reached into the back seat, extracted the bright yellow bag, and held it out. She could see the confusion cross his face.

I hope he likes it, Dad. She smiled. *See you soon.*

It was stupid to buy a puppet, she thought. What was I going to do with it anyway? But she regretted the loss of Pinocchio. The little liar. It had been a ridiculous thing to buy and an impulsive thing to give away. But she smiled to think of Tanner's face when he saw the puppet gambolling in mid-air, her father manipulating the strings so that it danced and moved. Surreptitiously switching the nose and making it grow for him. Vividly demonstrating the evils of lying and falsehoods.

He was definitely cute, she thought, and he was clearly comfortable with *her* grandparents. It was touching to see how they doted on him. And her father had been so gentle and tender. It made her wonder if he'd ever been that way with her mother, or with her. She couldn't remember, but she was tired and not calm. She had met her brother. He was real. Calculating quickly, she thought he must be turning four. It had been at least five years since her father had developed his *other interests*. And now she was back home. Her first year of teaching. Two degrees in between. Five years of dealing with her mother without the gentle buffer of her father.

THE FALL

Stella pulled into the driveway, turned off the ignition, and sat there for a moment gathering her composure. She had much to conceal. But when she walked in she knew at once that something was unusual. The TV was turned off and yet all the lights were ablaze. Her mother was not, as she'd anticipated, seated half asleep in the living room, nor was she in her bedroom. Stella strode through the house calling for her. She heard a moan from the bathroom and opened the door to see her mother in a pitiful heap on the floor.

What's wrong?

Where have you been? Pam sobbed. *I've been waiting for you.*

I was shopping in the city and stopped for dinner. What happened? Stella knelt beside her and began to feel her ankles and feet, cupping her hands and moving them gently up and down her limbs, trying to feel for a break or cut.

I fell on the floor, Pam whimpered, *and it hurt so much I couldn't get up. Everything hurts. I think I tripped on my housecoat.*

Is anything broken?

Everything is broken! I'm sick, and everything hurts all the time.

Let me help you up. Stella wedged her arm under her mother's twisted leg and placed her other arm around her hips. *I'm going to pull you gently, Mom, and you must grip the sink and try to help me stand.*

I can't do it, she said, *I'm too weak. You'll have to call someone.*

Let's try, first, Mom.

No, you'll just hurt me worse.

Stella looked at her critically. While Pam certainly looked uncomfortable, she didn't seem to be either pale or blotchy. There must be a way to get her up and into bed without disturbing anyone else. *Let's try first, shall we, Mom? Just one try?*

No! I won't try! You'll hurt me. Call an ambulance! Her mother pushed herself backwards on the floor and wedged herself under the sink, wrapping her arms around the pedestal and glaring at Stella defiantly. *You shouldn't have left me for so long. I'll be covered all over in bruises.*

Mom, let me get you a chair. I'll hold on to the back of it and you can try to raise yourself. Let's try once, before I make a fuss and call the ambulance. You won't want the neighbours thinking you've had a heart attack or something. Everyone will come rushing over and see you in your housecoat with no makeup.

Her mother considered for a moment and then nodded weakly, loosening her grip on the sink. *Just once. I'll try just the once.*

Stella left the bathroom and returned with a dining room armchair. *Move onto your knees, Mom, and I'll hold the back.* Pushing the chair towards her, Stella coaxed her into kneeling position and then gingerly helped her stand while leaning heavily on the chair. Her mother shrieked and sobbed by turn, impressing upon Stella the pain and discomfort she was experiencing. Stella led her gently down the hall to her bedroom and eased her into bed, covering her carefully and arranging the pillows as directed. Then she went to the kitchen and returned with the painkillers, the sleeping pills, a glass of water, and a mug of warm milk, administering these patiently.

Her mother gestured with her hand that Stella was dismissed. Stella sighed to herself and went about locking the doors, turning off the lights, lowering the thermostat, setting the house alarm. Then she stood outside Pam's room and listened to her steady breathing. The drugs would easily lull her mother into a deepened state. She wouldn't likely wake up before mid-morning.

SATURDAY

How funny, Stella thought, *that I'd worried about deceiving her when she's beyond having any real interest in my life*. She turned on her computer and sat down to check her email. In her inbox was a message from her father. She clicked on it apprehensively.

Stella, thank you for Tanner's birthday gift. I was glad to see you tonight. Love, Dad

It was a short email, but it required some sort of response. Otherwise he'd think she wasn't glad to have met Tanner. Stella began to compose a note.

Dad, Tanner is a really cute kid. I bet he's great. Mom had a fall while I was out. I found her on the bathroom floor. I guess she'd been there for a few hours. She's in bed sleeping now. Love, Stella.

Stella clicked send before looking it over. She didn't particularly feel like being careful.

Early the next morning there was another message.

Dear Stella, I'm sorry that Pam isn't well and that you're left to look after her. I guess the thing is, if she's unwell, we may need to talk about selling the house and putting her in an apartment. Think about what you really want to happen, Stella, and then tell me how I can help. Don't feel like you're stuck. Love, Dad

Stella walked slowly down the hall to the bathroom, got into the shower, and leaned wearily into the cascade. How easy he made it sound. Was it so easy for him? Is that how he'd managed to walk away?

As she soaped herself she planned the hours ahead: check Mom, make her breakfast, tidy the house, begin some marking, work out lunch and dinner, run to the grocery store, make Pam tea, call her doctor for an appointment, more marking, do a load of laundry, organize her school outfits for the week, check her bank balance, respond to her father's email. Seven-thirty in the morning and the day seemed daunting, the demands unremitting. Surely to God there was a better way.

Stella emerged from the steamy stream and towelled herself dry. Then she reread her father's email and considered his words. *Don't feel like you're stuck.*

Pam was asleep in her mint green and white bedroom. Everything was in shades of the same green: the carpet, the walls, the drapes. Pam even had a collection of nightgowns in mint green silk, trimmed luxuriously with fine ecru lace. She was wearing one of these now and seemed to blend into the soft green bedding, disappearing in the muted hues. The flash of her rings was the only thing that captured the light and sustained any energy. Beside her on the bureau was a stack of Harlequin Romances, an assortment of pill bottles and naturopathic tinctures, and a box of Kleenex covered in crocheted acrylic that resembled a green poodle. Her breathing was even and still. No obvious pain or discomfort marred her face. For the moment, all was well.

PAM AND STELLA

Stella rummaged through the fridge and cupboards and then began constructing peanut butter and cream-cheese cracker sandwiches, piling a plate with a dozen or more. A can of cola completed her breakfast, eaten cross-legged on the floor in front of the television with the sound carefully muted. She pondered the day. Something fun, she thought. She needed to get out and do something fun, if only she could think of what that might be.

On impulse she left a message for Tara. She would let Tara direct her; Tara was usually game for anything. Maybe she could forgo the marking and squeeze in a movie or some shopping. Whatever Tara wanted. No matter what.

She felt short of breath. The house was too hot. She turned the thermostat down further; Pam would never know. The furnace sighed, the fan clicked off, and for a moment Stella felt in harmony with the house. Guiltily, she slunk down the hall to check on Pam: still sleeping. Then, finally, Tara called back. *Sure. Pick you up at eleven.* Thank God. An escape plan.

Hi Dad, Not sure. Going out with Tara. Mom still resting. Thanks. Love, Stella.

That would do for now.

At ten Stella woke her mother with a breakfast tray. *I hurt too much to eat,* Pam protested. After some gentle persuasion, she condescended to taste the egg and nibble a piece of toast. *It doesn't taste right. I don't have any taste buds left.*

It's only because you've taken your medicine, Mom. It will come back. I'm going out with Tara for a while. Do you want me to bring you back anything?

Going out? How could you leave me like this? Don't you care what happens to me? Pam flung herself back against the pillows and began to snivel.

Mom, I need to get a few things. I'll be back in time to make a nice dinner. Promise. Stella picked up the tray and steeled herself for the inevitable.

Do what you want—I don't need you. I don't need anybody. Not your father and certainly not you.

I'll be home by four. I'll leave a sandwich for you on the counter. Stella slipped out of the room and headed back to the kitchen. Swearing quietly, she cursed by turns the can opener, the tuna tin, the crisper drawer in the fridge, the wax paper. *Damn. Fucket. Bullshit. Gawdamn fucken bullshit.*

Tara pulled into the driveway early, but Stella was waiting for her, coat on and ready.

So, where to?

I don't care. Anywhere. Just away.

How 'bout the mall? I could use some pantyhose.
Great.
Tara backed the car out. *You okay?*
I think I may have hit my limit.
What happened?
As they drove Stella told her all about meeting Tanner and how strange it had been and then how she'd found Pam when she got home and then her father's emails. Then she launched into a litany of complaints about her mother that she knew Tara had already heard but would patiently listen to again.

. . . And I know I'm a horrible person for talking about her this way, Stella wound up, *but sometimes I feel like I just can't stand it anymore. I'll probably go to hell.*

Stop. You're not a horrible person and you don't even believe in hell. Your mother is a piece of work. She always has been. It's not your fault your dad left. Crap. It's not even your dad's fault he left. She's totally self-absorbed. She drove him out. And if she's not careful, she'll lose you too.

Tara! Don't say stuff like that. I feel guilty enough.

It's true, for God's sake. How much can a person take? Tell me, how many doctors does she have?

Tara. Stop.

No, really. Consider. A family doctor, an eye doctor, a dentist, a doctor for her arthritis. Anyone else?

And an ortheo-something who realigns her neck and shoulders. Okay. You're right. There's a lot.

No one has that many doctors. At two appointments each, per month, she'd be out every other day. She probably keeps busy just making appointments.

Stop. I get it. I just don't know what to do about it.

You gotta leave. Let's get a place together. You know I've been saving for a down payment. So there's that new subdivision being built north of town. Townhouses. I went through a model home a week ago. And it's perfect—I'll tell you all about it. But for now: go in with me.

I can't.
Why not?

Who'd do the grocery shopping and mow the lawn and shovel the walkway?

Stella, you can spend your whole life looking after her, and you know what, it won't make you happy. And it sure as hell won't make Pam happy. It won't even make her well. She won't be grateful, either. She won't look at you when she's dying and say, "Stella, you were a wonderful daughter." Shit. She'll probably just tell you that it's about time you did something with your hair.

STELLA'S PASSION

Tara insisted on visiting some pop-ups to try on ridiculous dresses. Neither bought anything, but Tara was so entertaining as she slipped in and out of the confections and modelled them in confident runway swaggers that it made Stella laugh and lifted her out of herself.

Her mother was lying on the living room couch when she walked in. *How are you, Mom?*

My neck has been spasming all day. I tried an ice pack for my shoulder but it didn't work.

Did you call the doctor?

What's the point? They can't do anything. I just have to suffer.

Did you have lunch?

A little. It hurt to chew. Did you buy anything?

No. Can I make you some tea?

Yes. Tea might be good. But not too hot.

Stella picked up the ice bag and the plate, trudged to the kitchen, and returned to her thoughts. Was Tara right? Would her mother just use her up? Was that the way to spend her life—trying to please Pam? Trying to make amends for something she'd had no part in?

She began the tea and then pulled out a frozen roast for dinner. The kitchen cupboard housed their small inventory of alcohol. The sherry bottle was usually at the front, but Stella couldn't find it. *Mom, do you know where the sherry is? I thought I'd cook a roast.*

There isn't time for a roast, Stella. Don't you know anything? They take hours to cook slowly. Besides, I don't know where your stupid sherry is.

Stella popped the roast back in the freezer. Poached eggs and bacon for dinner, then. But where was the sherry? It was a new bottle, bought the weekend before. Maybe not. Maybe Stella had just intended to buy one and forgot. It was hard to keep track of all the little chores and errands Pam sent her on. These, on top of the housework and her marking and lesson prep, kept Stella busy. Busier than she'd like.

There was never time anymore to curl up with a good book and just read the whole thing from cover to cover. Stella longed sometimes for those days at U of T when she'd pulled on a cozy sweater and head over to the red leather couches at Hart House. What a wonderful way to spend a rainy afternoon. She'd even thought teaching would be like that. Luxurious amounts of time to sink into a novel and daydream. Time to wander the stacks, pulling out books whose spines looked well worn or interesting. Leather volumes with gilded pages. First editions and the rare books in Thomas Fisher. White gloves in place, gingerly examining the stylistic changes in punctuation made by editors in different editions of the same book. Dickens. Burns. Eliot. This was her real passion. The imposition of editorial decisions.

Her father got it. Besides her professors, he was one of the few people who understood, or at least respected, her interest in this meticulous work. And he encouraged it. *Maybe you'll become a great editor yourself someday, like Maxwell Perkins at Scribner's. Maybe you'll discover another Hemingway or Fitzgerald. Why not try to get a job with a big publishing house? Or maybe do a degree in library science?*

Stella couldn't imagine herself becoming a great anything, but this wasn't something she'd ever said to anyone. She was in awe of people with confidence. Great-looking women who could walk into a room and be the centre of attention. Many of her students had this strange air, this wow factor, that made them exciting and charismatic. They weren't the smartest kids, or the most attractive, or the richest; they were just confident. It was a magical thing to watch. The student council co-president, the star in the school show, the MVP athlete. There were so many things that seemed mysterious to Stella.

She'd taken to waking up once or even twice during the night with a full-blown panic attack. She'd be gasping for breath, her heart pounding, her skin damp. It had been happening on and off for months now. And during the day, if she found herself in small spaces, the sense of being suffocated would come over her. She'd have to stand near an opened window and inhale deep breaths of fresh air until her breathing calmed. In and out. In and out. In through the nose. Out through the mouth.

Stella had told no one about these attacks. Tara would blame her mother. Her father would blame her job. Her grandparents would just worry. Her doctor was also Pam's doctor and she didn't want him drawing any conclusions. Nor was she prepared to take any meds. This thing had started on its own and it needed to be controlled and go away on its own. That's all there was to it. There couldn't be two sickly people in one household.

She'd disciplined herself to stay calm, to focus on those things she could control. In the evenings, she'd often read and reread some of her papers from university, basking in the comments scribbled by her professors on the bottom of the pages. She'd been told that her particular interest in editorial punctuation was an unexplored field and that she should continue her work at the graduate level.

A paper she'd written on Burns and the Kilmarnock edition had been deemed publishable by her professor, who'd suggested she send it out to journals. Stella would often reread that paper in particular, marvelling at her own research and insight. She found it exciting to remember that she'd created it—she'd come up with the hypothesis and then set out to prove it. She'd been able to track down multiple examples of inconsistencies in line breaks and punctuation over subsequent editions to demonstrate her point. It was quite brilliant, really. She hugged this accomplishment to herself, knowing it would remain her original scholarly work, and her secret.

CALIFORNIA

Pam was alone in the house again. It was hard to be so much alone. Stella lived with her but was never there. She was either at school or with Tara or visiting her grandparents. What good was it to have a daughter if she never wanted to spend any time with you? Thank God she had the television to keep her company. She used to have friends who would call her up and talk, but for some reason they had all stopped. She had their phone numbers somewhere in an address book, but if they didn't want to call her, why should she call them? Busybodies anyway. Full of gossip and news. Always asking questions. Who cares about their boring lives? She and these women had had their children together, walked them to school together, and met for coffee sometimes during the day, but those times were gone. The children were grown. Most of them at university or married or working. Like Stella. Now they didn't have so much in common.

When she hadn't been so sick, Pam had dreamed of going to California. Not to live, just to visit. To shop on Rodeo Drive. To be transformed into a stunning beauty. And to tour the studios! Those glorious studios where her favourite movies were made. MGM, Twentieth-Century Fox, Columbia Pictures, Universal Pictures. She'd heard there were bus tours to the homes where the stars lived.

Why William had never wanted to take her, Pam didn't know. He was so boring. So predictable. Except for those damn rugs of his. She'd always known he was crazy for those rugs. He liked them more than he liked people. She'd pretended to be interested in them, but she couldn't have cared less. Especially when she found out how much they cost. The amount of money for one of those rugs would've paid for a trip to California. But he never wanted to go. It's not that he was cheap with money; he'd said *she* could go, but who wants to go to California by themselves? He just didn't understand. She tried to tell him what he was missing, how other people lived, but he was happy with his rugs and his predictable little life.

Stella wasn't interested either. Pam had tried to engage her, but she always preferred to read a book or listen to stories from her grandparents. The same stories over and over again. How bad it was. How much death they saw. Such suffering. Such fear. Who wants to hear that crap all the time? What does it matter so many years later? Everybody is safe. Why should it matter anymore?

What would it be like to actually live in a place like California, Pam wondered. A place so bright and sunny, so rich and beautiful, that no one was touched by the dark shadow lurking behind all that was done. No bars on the windows, no tins in the basement, no money saved in jam jars. And no fear that it wasn't over—that another wave of hatred and violence was just around the corner, inching slowly forward, gathering strength and power. In California there were palm trees and wide streets, boulevards planted with exotic flowers. Birds of paradise planted in beds a mile long. She'd seen clips on television.

Pam thought she'd fit in well in California. She'd go to a tanning salon and get a nice bronze glow. She'd have a pedicure and a manicure. Bright pink nail polish with a hard topcoat so that it would last. She'd get the works: bikini wax, leg wax, moustache wax. She'd ask them to check for stray hairs on her chin. Eyebrow threading. Then she would shop. A brightly coloured summer dress with matching clutch and bright shoes. The brighter the better. Big sunglasses. She could still pull it off. No reason why not.

She could make heads turn if she went to California. William might not notice her anymore, but there were lots who would. Men would turn to watch her gently swaying hips as she sauntered along the boulevard, stopping to bend over the exotic flowers to pick one for herself. They'd admire the tight curve of her bottom while she bent down. Take in the look of her long legs in their heels. Yes, men would still want her. She could still be attractive to someone. But not here. Not in Waldham. Only in a place like California where the air was warm and dry and the climate good for her health. She wouldn't be sick in California. She'd be young again, with energy and a zest for life. She'd go to restaurants and shows and have friends in the movie business. She'd meet stars at parties. Life would be so different there.

SEDUCTION

How had she ended up in Waldham with an orthodontist who didn't love her and a daughter who didn't understand her? This was not how it was supposed to have worked out. It was Tony Dinapoli who'd been responsible. That stupid Italian loser. It was all his fault. That lovely black hair with the big curls on the top of his forehead, his dark brown eyes, his strong, muscled arms. The cigarettes he smoked like a rock star. His leather jacket and jeans. How could any girl resist a boy who looked like Tony?

He'd said he loved her. They were in High Park, lying under a lilac bush. He begged her for a touch. Just her bare skin, under her clothes. *A touch*, she thought, *how can a little touch be a sin?* But the next night he wanted more. He wanted to look and to touch. And then to taste. To lick her, and kiss her forcefully. He aroused her until she was so wet and her legs so weak that she couldn't stop him from doing all he desired. And for a moment, swept into the passion of his need, she wanted it too. But it hurt. He ripped her. She felt the tearing but when she whimpered he didn't stop. He pushed at her hard, with a furious energy and intention she hadn't anticipated. Afterwards, he laughed. *That wasn't so bad, was it?*

But it was bad. She knew it was bad. A carnal sin.

Do you love me?

Sure. He stood to pull out his cigarettes and light one. *Sure.*

But the next night he didn't come. She waited at the lilac bush until dusk. He didn't come the next night or the night after that, and then she knew he wouldn't come again. And that she had to make a plan. She couldn't tell her parents, she couldn't tell her friends, she couldn't tell the priest. If she was ruined, there must be someone who could help her.

She looked for Tony in the neighbourhood. The diner. The pool hall. The convenience store where he bought his smokes. She didn't see him and she didn't see his friends, either: Leo, Tomas, Josef. They had all disappeared. It was as if they'd conspired to make Tony invisible and untrappable. If she went to confession would the priest make Tony marry her? Or would he berate her? It preoccupied Pam for days. She waited to see if she'd run into Tony, and she waited for her monthly staining.

When it didn't come, when she didn't see him, she acted. She climbed the stairs to the third floor and entered William's room when he was in the bath. She made him the father of the baby Tony had planted inside her. It was easy to fool William. He took such pleasure in her body. He didn't ask questions or make her talk about her feelings. He just responded to her body. Once a week for three weeks and he was ready to marry her, to claim responsibility. It could have been his. Who knows.

Stella is weird like William, she thought. *Did his seed overtake Tony's and make the baby his? Was that possible? Did she lose Tony's baby and get pregnant with William's at the same time?* She'd read in one of her magazines that this was possible. So maybe it all worked out. Maybe Stella was William's daughter after all. She didn't look like him, but these things happen in families. Babies come out with green eyes and red hair even when their fathers have blond hair and blue eyes. Such things happen all the time. William never suspected.

Once, when she was visiting her parents, she took Stella out in the stroller. Stella was maybe three months old. She was walking her through the park, along the path, when she passed *the* lilac bush. She stopped and looked around carefully. Stared at the ground. Closed her eyes. Remembered the passion, the tearing, the pain. *Do you love me?* she'd asked. *Sure,* he'd said. *Sure.*

William wouldn't do such a thing, she said to herself quietly. *He is a man of honour. He wouldn't leave a girl like that.*

And that realization made Pam appreciate William in a new way. He wasn't just a fool easily tricked. He'd saved her from certain disgrace and shame and ruin. He had rescued her. He had fathered her child. That was the way it must be remembered. He was Stella's father.

TONY

Y*ou're in trouble, man. What if she's knocked up? Her old man is crazy.*

Yeah, they say he's got machine guns in his basement. You've seen the metal blinds. It's like a fortress. He's crazy as batshit. He'll kill you.

What should I do? I really like her but I'm not ready for no kid or anything.

Get the hell out of town, man. Split while you can.

My uncle said there's lots of work in Sudbury. He told me I should come and work for him in construction. We should all go.

I feel bad just leaving like this. Should I call her first?

You crazy? No way, man. We just gotta get out while we can.

THE MAGIC CARPET RIDE

Pam had a sense of commitment to William. Or at least to being a proper wife. She read magazines and decorated the house according to the latest trends. She bought throw pillows and tossed them on the couch for a splash of colour. She filled vases with flowers from their garden. She clipped recipes and experimented with casseroles and baked chicken. She changed her clothes before he came home each night, putting on a sexy outfit and fresh lipstick. She bought see-through lingerie trimmed with fake feathers and walked around in these until he grabbed her and pulled her down on the bed. She mixed him martinis. She made sure that when Stella cried in the night William's sleep wasn't interrupted. She did everything the magazines told her she should do.

And still he stopped listening to her stories. Stopped noticing her breasts cupped in lacy push-up bras, stopped caressing her with anything other than absent-minded habit and ritual. Somehow he just stopped. Everything stopped. He didn't grow hard and push her against the shower wall when she undressed beside him in the bathroom. He didn't reach for her in bed and roll over on her, breathing deeply with his need. He didn't notice the lingerie or the lipstick. He didn't even drink the martinis.

It must have been the damn rugs. Somehow a genie had woven a spell into them and called his name: *William, there is more to life than Waldham, than Pam, than Stella. Take a magic carpet ride and follow me.* And so he left Waldham, he left her, he left Stella, and went in search of something she could not name. The magazines didn't tell her what to do. They didn't list "magic carpets" as a reason for dying marriages. They advised *putting spice in the kitchen and spice in the bedroom.* She'd read all the articles, taken all the quizzes, tried all the advice. But William followed the carpets.

THE STARS

Pam developed her own interests. Elizabeth Taylor, Grace Kelly, Katherine Hepburn, and Doris Day were among the greats she studied from the Golden Age of Hollywood. She began a scrapbook for each one, pasting in magazine photos and articles and movie reviews. She filled out recipe cards with the names of movies they'd starred in. Pam developed a little system for her cards: placing a gold star by the name of her favourite films, a silver star by her second favourite, a red star by the ones she hadn't yet seen. The red stars were carefully scraped off and exchanged for a silver or gold when she'd seen the film and made a decision about it.

When Stella was small she'd sometimes help with the scrapbooks, finding her a glue stick or offering to draw a flowered border around a picture or article. Pam encouraged this. The girl spent far too much time reading and needed to appreciate the world that her mother could show her. Stella really was a mystery as she grew older. How could such a plain girl be so uninterested in sprucing herself up, making the most of what little she had? Pam would offer to do her nails or perm her hair but Stella always said *No, I don't want to sit that long.* And yet she'd certainly sit that long when she was reading a book. It just didn't make sense. It was unnatural, really. A girl who didn't want to be pretty.

Elizabeth Taylor was a beauty. What Pam wouldn't give for her violet eyes and pale skin. Doris Day was perky and cute. The most memorable thing about Doris was her costumes: always the most stylish, the most modern, and in the best colours. Hollywood really knew how to dress Doris Day. Princess Grace was another matter; she was in a league of her own. No one could dispute that she was truly beautiful. If Pam had to choose between Elizabeth Taylor and Princess Grace, she wouldn't be able. It wasn't possible, really. Grace was feminine and classy whereas Elizabeth was passionate and sensuous. How could you choose between two such beauties? Who would want to?

Katherine Hepburn was different again. Spunky and interesting with a husky voice and long, elegant cigarettes. She was smart as opposed to beautiful. Pam knew she was nothing like Katherine. But Elizabeth, with her colouring, maybe a little? She could definitely darken and shape her brows to look like Liz, and Pam knew she already had a good little figure and well-shaped lips. But the light complexion: that was the problem. She'd tried rubbing half lemons on her face and hands and hair each morning after the shower. Her hair did appear to be shinier for the trouble, but her olive skin did not in any way show signs of becoming paler. She bought liquid foundation two shades lighter than her skin at the drugstore, and sometimes in the evening when she was dressing up for William she'd carefully rub it in, line kohl around her eyes and eyebrows, and apply dark red lipstick. Sometimes William noticed. Mostly he didn't.

Pam often wondered what William wanted. She did everything her mother did for her father, and everything the magazines told her good wives do. She wasn't unattractive. She liked sex and was happy to experiment with him in the bedroom. What more was there? But sometimes the tiniest doubt would creep into her head and she'd ask herself, *What's missing?*

It was the same with Stella. She looked after her. Saw that she was nicely dressed and well fed. But there was no sense that she'd die of grief if anything happened to her. Sometimes Pam would play a game with herself. She'd stand at the corner watching Stella join her friends as they walked to school and she'd say to herself, *That car, that car is going to hit her and she's going to die.* She'd work herself up and squeeze out some tears. She'd imagine the hospital, the church, the funeral. She'd plan the flowers, the outfit she would wear. She'd even stand before the bathroom mirror and make her face look stricken, overcome by grief. Practising her devastation. It wasn't that she *wanted* the car to hit Stella; she just wondered what it would feel like to have Stella deeply matter.

For Christmas one year, William gave her a biography of Elizabeth Taylor. She was impressed that he'd bought something so carefully selected to please. His other gifts had been showy and expensive: a gold bracelet, a Royal Doulton figurine, a velour housecoat. That same Christmas William gave Stella a very large telescope. The two of them spent much of the day assembling and calibrating it. *This way, you can both learn more about the stars,* he'd joked. Stella had laughed, but Pam didn't think it was very funny.

CLEOPATRA

Stella was still in high school when her mother went through her Elizabeth Taylor–Cleopatra phase. Equipped with a rented VCR from the library, Pam had watched and rewatched the movie until Stella was sure she'd memorized the entire script. In an effort to interest her, Pam had bought them matching bracelets and sandals and pale, diaphanous scarves for draping on their heads. At first Stella had willingly joined in. But after several days of the same film, the same dress-up routine, the same no-interruptions rule, Stella grew bored and began to make excuses.

Undeterred, Pamela added black eyeliner and a broad gold belt to her growing inventory. Stella came home from school one day to find Pam bent over the sewing machine, worrying a gauzy orange piece of fabric out from underneath the presser foot. Pam looked up and announced she was making Stella a Cleopatra out-fit for the Halloween dance. Both knew that Stella would never wear it.

It seemed that the more absorbed Pam became with Elizabeth Taylor's life, the more she began to mirror all aspects of the star. Liz drank; Pam drank. Liz was known for her exuberant sensuality; Pam adopted low-cut, tight-fitting tops and was never without full makeup and fragrance. Liz was seen wearing a silk caftan and scarf tied around her hair; Pam began wearing them too, wrapping the matching sashes around her head. Stella took to flipping through her mother's latest *Classics Hollywood* magazine to predict the new Liz look Pam would be sporting.

The Cleopatra costume, when it was finished, was a very respectable copy of an outfit Liz wore in the movie. Stella instead went off to the Halloween dance encased in a large cardboard box meant to represent one half of a pair of dice. Pam herself wore the Cleopatra costume, complete with makeup, to hand out candy to trick-or-treaters. William raised an eyebrow that evening when she sashayed into the living room, but assured her that she *looked just like Liz*. The magic words. Pam swayed her hips and waved her arms in an attempt at belly dancing. William smiled, applauded, and beat a hasty retreat to the basement.

Alone in the room now, Pam went over to the stereo and selected a record of Persian music she'd bought. Leaving the front door open, she cranked up the volume and continued to dance. Hours later, a number of unsuspecting fathers who'd accompanied their trick-or-treaters reported home and remarked on Mrs. Wheeler's attire to their more conventionally dressed wives. She was the subject of much discussion in the neighbourhood. Pam couldn't have cared less. Caught up in the music and a whirl of emotion, she'd felt, for that one evening, mysterious and exotic and captivating.

When the shelling out was completed and Stella had returned home, Pam turned off the porch light, locked the door, and went downstairs. William, comfortably ensconced in a recliner, was reading a book on Persian carpets. She pulled a silk scarf around his neck and grabbed at his hands, trying to entice him to get up and dance with her. He stood good-naturedly, but after a moment he looked so uncomfortable that Pam altered her approach. *Kiss me*, she beckoned, *kiss me as though you were Caesar*.

William pecked her on the lips but then sat down again in his recliner. Pam settled on his lap and began to undo his shirt buttons. *Make love to me*, she whispered, kissing the base of his throat, stroking his shoulders and arms. *Let's make love, here, on a carpet.*

Uh-uh, said William, abruptly changing the mood. *We can't risk staining it. Why don't you go upstairs and I'll join you later.*

I can't believe it, snapped Pam. *You care more about staining those damn rugs than you do about me. Here I am, throwing myself at you, and you're just worried about the carpets. What the hell is the point of having the stupid things if we can't ever use them for anything? Unbelievable.* She stomped off upstairs, scrubbed off her makeup, and cast aside her carefully constructed costume. Then she locked their bedroom door. William had to sleep in the guest room that night.

Over the next weeks William gradually moved his things into the guest room. He knew he'd wounded Pam and tried to apologize. He bought her roses. He said *I'm sorry for being insensitive.* He offered to take her out to a nice restaurant *to make it up to you.* He stopped by the jewellery store in the plaza and bought her a tiny emerald cocktail ring. Pam accepted his gifts and his apologies but maintained a hurt, aloof distance.

Stella tiptoed around them. She felt terrible for her father, who looked uneasy and dispirited, but didn't dare openly sympathize. Instead she shot him discreet glances that she hoped would convey *I love you but I'm afraid to say a word.* She also made herself agreeable to her mother, asking Pam to set her hair in hot rollers and allowing her to shape it into soft waves before school. She even allowed Pam to pluck her eyebrows, enduring a bathroom lecture on how her "uni-brow" was so pronounced that it needed regular attention. Stella later sat through a manicure, a leg waxing, and a facial.

Pam, for her part, was heartened that Stella with her dull complexion, dry hair, and chewed cuticles had finally let her to do what she did best: add some needed glamour and style to the dowdy. It had seemed such a waste to be dismissive of the pampering and care that real beauty required. Pam had felt as though she'd failed as a mother. Now she might make some real headway.

THE MAKEOVER

Transforming Stella into an attractive, more polished-looking girl became Pam's new focus. Stella had good marks. But without good looks and without boys, she was limited: destined to be a lonely frump with a good job.

Her first move was to inform William that she'd be taking Stella to Yorkdale mall and needed a lot of money to update her wardrobe. William handed over the chequebook and told her to spend what was needed. Then, withdrawing to his small office, he sat thoughtfully for some time.

Pam told Stella that they'd be going shopping early Saturday morning. Stella was a little surprised but readily agreed. *Wear something easy,* cautioned Pam. *Something you can pull off and on really quickly. You'll have a lot to try on.*

Stella made an effort. Setting aside her usual jeans and running shoes, she put on a pair of navy dress pants and a cotton blouse. Then she rummaged through her closet and found a pair of navy shoes with a slightly clunky heel that weren't too uncomfortable. Her mother smiled to see her *nicely dressed, for a change.*

Pam parked the car near the main entrance to the mall. Then she outlined her plan. *We'll start looking at this end and work our way along to the other end. Then we'll decide what we want and buy it on our way back to the car.*

Why not just buy what we like when we see it?

Because you don't want to pay too much. And you don't want to buy something everyone is wearing. You want classic pieces that demonstrate taste and style. Nothing too trendy or flamboyant.

Oh God, Mom, how much are we talking about? I thought you meant a new dress or two.

We need to replace your entire wardrobe. Including your underwear. It's time you started wearing proper foundation pieces. You can never start too early. You don't want things to start to sag.

They began in Eaton's lingerie department. Skin tone. Pam flipped expertly through the racks and selected bras with light foam padding, panties, and a couple of slips. Stella took them obediently into the fitting room but didn't bother trying them on. Instead she sat on the little gilt stool for what seemed an appropriate amount of time and then rejoined her mother. *Everything's fine, Mom, thanks.* Pam smiled delightedly and took the small mound to the cashier.

Next up were shoes and handbags. They emerged into the mall and gazed at the dancing bronze figures in the fountain. *Just a minute, Mom, let's make a wish.* Reaching into her purse, Stella pulled out two pennies and handed one to her mother. Each made a wish before tossing in the coins. Stella wished that her parents would make up and be happy and that the shopping trip would soon be over. That was two wishes, but perhaps the gods would listen regardless. Pam wished for something unexpected to happen in her life.

At the shoe store, Pam chose a pair of low caramel-coloured pumps with a matching purse and black high heels with a matching clutch bag. Stella flopped down on a fabric cube and dutifully stuck out her feet. She annoyed Pam by insisting on a caramel pump for one foot and a black high heel for the other, and then limped around the store deliberately. The forty-something salesman, dressed in a sober grey suit with a bright tie, smiled wryly but assured Pam that both shoes were a good fit. *They're great, Mom. Thanks.*

Despite Stella's antics, Pam was pleased with the selections. Plus, the salesman was both courtly and conversational. Pam thought he had exquisite taste and admired his boldly striped tie out loud while lightly touching the sleeve of his jacket. Stella was appalled to see her mother flirting.

Back in the mall, she pointed at a store she actually liked and suggested they go there next. Pam recoiled. *Stella, the point of today isn't to buy more of what you already have.* Stella sighed and tried not to lose her cool. Jeans and T-shirts were comfortable. It's what all her friends wore. What was the big deal? By now Pam had moved to an expensive boutique with a display rack of woollen blazers outside the front entrance. She held up a bright yellow one. Stella shook her head. Pam held up a bright green one. Stella shook her head. Pam chose a navy blue one and held it out. Stella put it on.

Looking at herself in the glass storefront, she said, *It's great, Mom. How about this?*

No. Not enough style.

I like it, said Stella hopefully.

Stella, you have to listen to me. It has no pizzazz. We'll keep looking.

Stella sighed again, but took off the blazer and rehung it. She followed her mother to the next ladies' store, where Pam was already riffling through the racks and picking out dresses. Stella agreed to try on *four only,* let Pam choose which ones, and then went into the dressing room and pulled a dress on over her pants. It fit. She went out to show her mother.

Stella, go back at once and take off those pants. How can I tell if it fits properly when it's bunched up over your slacks?

Stella went back and removed her pants, forcing herself to remember that this trip was about humouring Pam and helping her dad. Then she swaggered out, hands on hips, and struck a pose for her mother. Pam was pleased with the dress and sent Stella back to try on another. Finally she asked the saleswoman to hold two of the dresses for a couple of hours while they continued shopping. Stella didn't much like either of them but thought the green was less offensive than the pink. She didn't say a word.

Pam seemed energized now, and as they continued down the mall she showed Stella a list she'd drawn up of necessary purchases: four tops, two pants, two skirts, two dresses, one blazer, shoes and purses. Stella felt her stomach clutching in that strange, sick *Are you well enough prepared?* belly-flop thing it always did before a presentation or exam. She told herself that if they could just wrap up this endless shopping, she'd agree to wear anything.

They went straight to another department store, where, to Stella's relief, lots of options met Pam's criteria. Stella helped her choose a navy blazer, a matching navy wrap-around skirt, a pleated skirt, and an assortment of tops. She obediently carried these things to the fitting room and modelled them for her enthusiastic mother. Then, while Stella was dressing, Pam wandered off and disappeared into the evening wear section. Stella found her there admiring a lemon yellow gown printed with vibrant purple flowers.

Stella waxed eloquently on the tulips and suggested that Pam try it on.

Oh, I don't need to try it on. I know the brand name, and this is my perfect size.

Great. Let's get it. I'm sure Dad won't mind.

Yes, I think I will.

Listen, why don't I go look at the accessories while you pay for this stuff and then we'll be done. Pam happily agreed. Minutes later she joined Stella in the costume jewellery department and helped her choose some beads and belts that would add a *splash of colour* to her new clothes.

Stella could not believe her good fortune. It was only two o'clock, and except for the backtracking, they appeared to be finished. She was so relieved that she hugged her mother and thanked her profusely for everything.

DÉTENTE

When William came home from the clinic that night he found the table set for dinner. Pam, dressed unaccountably in a yellow and purple floor-length gown with an apron over top, was preparing fried chicken: his favourite. Stella, looking only slightly sullen, was made to model several new outfits carefully accessorized with new shoes and scarves and jewellery. William was amused at his ungainly daughter's attempts to please her mother. It was touching. At his place at the table was an Eaton's bag with two new dress shirts and a pair of striped ties.

A couple of your shirts were getting frayed collars, said Pam, *and we decided you needed a treat, too.*

William thanked his wife and crossed the room to give her a peck on the cheek. He winked at Stella, thankful that peace had been restored.

The goodwill and bonhomie were short-lived. Stella was to find herself terrorized every time she pulled on her jeans and started to leave the house. *You don't appreciate the trouble I've gone to* became the newest of Pam's refrains. Stella made a concerted effort to throw on a blazer, insert a pair of earrings, or wrap a scarf around her neck, but these half-hearted attempts seemed only to highlight her deficiencies. William kept himself removed, trying conspiratorially to encourage Stella when they had a moment alone.

PAMELA AND THE STRANGER

Pamela was not a little put out by all the time Stella was spending away from home. She didn't appreciate having to do the grocery shopping by herself and had started to dislike highway driving. It was just so much easier when Stella did these things for her.

Pam was carefully driving down Waldham's main street looking for a parking spot. She hated angle parking and was hoping to find one of the few spaces on the street where you could parallel park. She didn't like parallel parking either, so what she really needed was a double parking spot that allowed her to glide into place without having to put the car in reverse. She just didn't understand why the Township didn't do something about the parking situation and make things easier for people.

Fortunately, at the end of the strip Pam was able to locate a place to her liking. It meant having to walk farther, but at least she wouldn't have to worry about reversing out onto the street later. Her first errand was at the bank. She wanted to update her bank book and withdraw grocery money for the week.

She looked around at the other customers while she waited for her turn. A young man in a grey three-piece suit was standing by the manager's office, speaking earnestly to someone she couldn't see. She gazed at him in shock, her body electrified. Something about him was so familiar that her skin broke out in tiny goosebumps. She couldn't place him at first. Was it possible? Could it really be? The same hair, the same build. But in a suit? In Waldham? And how could he still look so young? Could it be a son or a double, or were her eyes playing tricks on her? Pam stared at him boldly until he looked up at her. She continued to stare. He nodded politely and then looked away.

Pam moved up in the line. She was stunned. A face from the past, a precious memory. Her face was burning. She felt as though someone had reached into the place where she buried her secrets and exposed them for all of Waldham to see. Feeling the need to check that she was fully clothed, she looked down at her dress and patted the fabric, smoothing it over her slender hips. Then she touched her hair, flattening it gently and then fluffing it with her fingers. The stranger in the grey suit walked past her quickly, striding purposefully out the door. Pam hesitated, turned her head, and watched him leave.

THE DIVORCE

Pam believed that she was doing the right thing by Stella and that she was a good wife to William. She was astonished, then, when William announced one night that he'd developed *other interests*. He'd met the woman at some Persian rug convention; she worked for one of the many importing houses he dealt with for his damn carpets. She'd also published articles on the social significance of Persian carpets and their origins. Hoity toity. Big deal. So she was smart. She had no business stealing someone else's husband.

You expected your parents to be sympathetic and to take your side. Instead her father blamed her, saying that she should have tried harder to make William happy. Her mother sighed quietly. *You were always a bit selfish, Pamela, and there is no room for selfish in a marriage.* Their words scorched her. She vowed never to go to them ever again no matter what she was dealing with. How dare they blame her for this? He was the one who fell in love with that damn carpet woman. He was the one who left her on some sort of magic carpet ride.

THE NAZI

Stella was enjoying her Saturday morning reading the newspaper before her mother wakened. Paper flattened and arranged in sequence on the breakfast table. Coffee with cream in a large mug. Buttered toast. The decadence of this solitary self-indulgence filled Stella with a deep sense of quiet. But then she saw the news item. A small column.

ALBERT AACHEN FOUND LIVING IN QUIET TORONTO SUBURB. *Aachen was recently tracked down by American Nazi-hunter Avrom Mueller. Aachen, 78, is a retired tool and die maker. His modest Runnymede house is surrounded by rose beds, and his neighbours say that he is "always willing to help with a project." Aachen is wanted for the gruesome 1942 murder of 1,728 Jews, who were rounded up and forced into a synagogue near Antwerp, Belgium. Under his orders, they were executed by a firing squad and the synagogue torched. Before the mass execution, Aachen, a highranking official with the Waffen SS hit squad, allegedly took infants from their mothers' arms and tossed them in the air, spearing them on his bayonet. Plans are underway for Aachen's extradition to The Hague, where he is expected to stand trial.*

She felt her chest draw tight. The "Nazi dog" Stan had once encountered in the park—was this the same man? How many Nazis could there still be? Did he have a wonky arm? Why wasn't there a picture? And had Stan seen the paper?

Seventy-eight. Aachen was seventy-eight. So was her grandfather. The coincidence was uncanny. How was it possible that two such different men should have crossed paths at least twice in their lives—once in the Netherlands in the deep of war and then here in High Park in the twilight of their lives? Both with secrets. Both sleepless, haunted by the memories of their past. Frightened that a button in history would somehow trigger replay and they'd once more be caught in the terror and the violence of that time.

Stan had been right. This was no figment of his imagination but rather a living fragment from another era. He lived quietly in the suburbs of Toronto. He had rose gardens. He fed ducks in

High Park. Did Aachen remember his past cruelties? Did he remember the screams from within the synagogue as rounds of ammunition were expended? The cries of frightened villagers in their night clothes, watching, teeth chattering, as their neighbours and friends were singled out for death. The flashes of cruel light, the smashing sounds of devastation, the echoes of firepower drilling insistently, ricocheting. The strong smell of warm urine as the terrified crowds wet themselves. How much did he allow himself to remember?

Did Aachen's wife know who he really was and what he'd done? Did she even suspect him? Had she glimpsed the inhumanity in him or tasted his cruelty? Or was his hatred spent now? Was he a good father? Was he loved? And how would Aachen's wife, and children if he had any, reconcile their experience of the man they knew with the newspaper reports? Would they attend his trial or would they shun him? Were they tainted by the stain of him? Was there a demon of inevitability that taunted them to recognize their twisted destiny?

Stella called her father. It was Saturday. Maybe he could meet her there. Maybe he'd have an insight that would calm her.

WILLIAM AND STELLA

William answered the phone on the first ring.
   Dad?

Stella? You okay?

Yes, I'm worried about Grandpa. Did you see the paper?

No, not yet. Why?

They arrested a Nazi war criminal living near High Park. He was right there, Dad. Grandpa was right. There are Nazis here.

Well, maybe, but maybe not. We don't know that for sure. Stan is old and tired and frightened. He sees what he wants to see. It could be a trick of his imagination. It doesn't mean that this is the same man. It doesn't even mean that this man is who they say he is.

A Nazi hunter tracked him down. They don't just make mistakes like that.

I'll read the article now. God. Maybe it is him. But one never knows. People, in their eagerness to do the right thing, often take short-cuts, they make assumptions, make mistakes.

Do you think Grandpa knows? Should we tell him?

Absolutely not. We don't want to frighten him. Let's visit. We'll see what he does know. But we won't tell him if we don't have to.

What about Grandma?

We'll see. Do you want to meet me there?

That would be great. I already told Mom I was going out this morning.

Okay. Let me do a few things first. It may take me a bit to get ready. I'll see if Tanner wants to come. I'll meet you there in about an hour, hour and a half.

Stella got in her car and sat for a moment. Discussing such things with her father had always been easy. But for now she'd keep this from Pam—she couldn't face her skepticism. She'd deal with her later, when she knew what was what.

The Parkway traffic was light and Stella made the drive in good time. It would be at least forty-five minutes before her father arrived. She pulled into a grocery store near her grandparents' place and navigated the aisles, looking for a treat to take them. Then she spotted something she'd never noticed before: Matchbox Dinky cars. Brightly coloured sports coupes in lime green, lemon yellow, neon blue. She chose two. Then, after finding a delicious-looking flan, she moved to the cash with a sense of satisfaction. Stella smiled boldly at the clerk who served her. She didn't often smile at strangers; mostly she looked down, as though she might be bothering someone. But today was differ-ent. Today, despite the horrible news, might be a good day.

When she got to the house she saw that her father had arrived before her. Had Tanner come too? She hoped so.

Maria came to the door right away and welcomed her as warmly as ever. Stella passed her the bag containing the flan but kept the other bag with her. It made her feel secure. Armed, per-haps. She was armed with a toy: a silly thought. But she wanted Tanner to like her; it was important. She'd never interacted with a small child before, and how these relationships worked was a mystery.

One look at her father's face and Stella knew it was bad. Her grandfather was lying down in his room. Stan *never* took naps and never lay in bed unless he was very sick. Tanner was seated cross-legged in front of the television, engrossed in a children's show.

Dad?

Her father walked over and gave her a gentle hug. *He already knows, Stella. It's all around the neighbourhood. He was having trouble breathing. Just anxiety. I made him lie down.*

What can we do?

I'm not sure. We'll see how he is when he wakes up. I might have to take him to the walk-in clinic. He may need something for his anxiety.

I brought something for Tanner, Stella blurted out. *Do you want it?*

No. You give it to him yourself. Wait till the show is over. He'll be happy with anything. It was good of you to think of him.

Do you think it's true, Dad? Could it be the same man?

Stranger things have happened, Stella. Your grandfather was pretty sure he recognized him. It's possible.

Stella paused. *Dad, do you take Tanner to visit your parents?*

They've met him. Once or twice maybe. They don't have a lot of time for visiting.

I wondered . . .

Are you asking about Fatima? He paused and waited for Stella to nod her head. *They've met her too. A couple of times. But they're busy people.*

Have Grandma and Grandpa met her?

Yes. Yes, they have. They came to our wedding, in fact. They've always been supportive. Why are you asking now?

I just wondered, Dad, why not me? Don't you think she'd like me?

Oh, God, Stella, no! It was never about Fatima not liking you. I was trying to protect you from being caught in the middle. I didn't think your mother would understand.

Stella nodded again. This made sense. *I'm sorry, Dad, for not asking sooner. And I'm sorry I didn't attend your wedding.*

PAM AND TONY

Thursday was Pam's regular appointment day with her family doctor. If she didn't need to see him that week she'd called his nurse, Nancy, and cancel. Otherwise, she had a standing 1:00 to 1:10 slot. It was convenient that way. Dr. Sheffer was patient with Pamela and managed to never make her feel like a bother. She'd tried flirting with him from time to time and had even worn a sexy bra, but he never seemed to notice. Anyway, he was old and had a pleasant dumpling of a wife.

Pam needed a refill on one of her meds, and although the pharmacy would have called the doctor for her, she decided she might as well drop in at the clinic to collect it. She was in the waiting room when she noticed a man sitting in the corner watching her. He looked to be her age but was dressed like a teenager in running shoes and a tracksuit. *How totally inappropriate*, thought Pam. *Adults should dress their age*. She looked down coyly, not entirely displeased that he was studying her. Today was a good day. She was wearing a nice green summer outfit with beige sandals. Her legs looked good for someone her age, she knew, and she had just painted her toes with fresh polish. Pam crossed her legs deliberately and ran her hand modestly over the fabric of her skirt.

Pam. The doctor can see you now. She stood up, smoothed her skirt again, and stepped forward. When she came out of Dr. Sheffer's office, prescription tucked carefully in her handbag, the man in the corner was standing.

Pam Lipinski! I knew you were familiar. It's me, Tony! Remember me?

She shuddered. Everything stopped. The piped-in music quieted, the receptionist ceased talking on the telephone, the entire waiting room froze. She looked at the man, his build, his thick, grey-streaked hair, his tanned face, his hands with their ropey cords and two large gold signet rings.

You must be mistaken, said Pam stiffly. *I don't remember you.*

Of course you do. He stepped closer. *I'm Tony, Tony Dinapoli, from the old neighbourhood.*

No, really, you're mistaken. She moved away from him, out of the waiting room and into the foyer. Tony followed.

Of course you remember me. We dated for a while, after high school. I took you to the park.

What are you doing here? What do you want? She was walking briskly to her car now, wishing she hadn't been so stupid and parked so far away. Tony was keeping pace, bounding alongside her good-naturedly.

I just moved here. With my son, Frankie. He's a big-shot real estate developer. So, you live here now?

What do you want, Tony? I'm pretty busy.

That's all the hello a guy gets, after all this time. You look good, Pam. How are you? You're lookin' very good, if I may say.

Pam stopped by her car. She was feeling flustered. She'd intended to stop at the drugstore but had walked right past it. *Thank you, Tony. Nice to see you. I have to go; I'm busy.*

Too busy for a cuppa coffee with an old friend? C'mon, let me buy you a coffee somewhere. We can talk. Catch up. You can tell me what you been doin' with yourself. Tony was bouncing back and forth on the soles of his running shoes, grinning at her. For a second, Pam had a glimpse of the younger Tony, the high-energy boy who never sat still, and she softened. He caught her eye. *Just a cuppa coffee. Give a guy a break, eh Pam, I don't know anyone in this town.*

She relented: *Not here. We'll have to drive. There's a little restaurant just outside of town on the highway. You can follow me. Where's your car?*

Over there, the black pickup.

Really?

Whaddya mean by that? It's just a little loaded.

Have you grown up at all, Tony?

Yeah, sure. I'm grown up. He tipped his chin a little defensively. *Now let's go.*

Pam drove to the tiny restaurant. It wouldn't do for too many people to see her having coffee with a man. Especially a man in a tracksuit. They might talk. She was panicked, though, and turned on her windshield wipers instead of her turn signal. She also drove too fast, trying to impress him. *This is foolish, really. Why am I even going?* She parked her car and waited. He drove in beside her, seemed to spring out of his truck, and then bounced around to her door and opened it. That was a surprise.

Hey sweetheart, he said to the waitress, *we need a nice quiet table in the corner. And lunch menus.* He winked at Pam.

Pam stared down at her hands awkwardly. She still wore her engagement ring, even though in a fit of pique she'd long since flushed her wedding band down the toilet. It had taken several flushes and a large wad of toilet paper to make it disappear. She was sorry afterwards and thought she should have offered the ring to Stella. Tony had picked up the vinyl menu and was reading it with interest.

I will just refuse to be awkward, thought Pam. *This is simply a casual encounter between two people from the same neighbourhood. I will manage this.*

Tell me about your son.

Frankie? Ah, Frankie's a good kid. He started out in construction, and before I knew it they was promoting him to front office. And then suddenly he's in real estate sales and now he's the goddamn project manager for a big housing development outside of town. The kid's got a horseshoe up his ass. He does all right for himself.

And you? What do you do?

Me? I'm a slouch. I don't do nothin' anymore.

What have you done? What was your profession?

Me? No profession. Just worked my ass off. A sawmill for a time. Then in the mines for a few years. Hated that shit. Then I got lucky and started selling used trucks. I bought a little dealership franchise with a couple of partners. I did all right.

Then what happened?

Well, we were living north, in Sudbury, and the roads are bad in the winter. Rita got herself killed on the highway one night and me, I started drinking. Almost drank the business away. My partners bought me out. But I kept a stake.

Pam leaned away from him a bit. *Oh?*

And then I got lucky again. Turns out the whole dealership thing was like a gold mine. I been living like a king ever since.

And the drinking?

I went to AA. Did the whole goddamn twelve steps. My doctor put me on pills that made me puke. He said I was embalming my liver and had to stop. So I did. Pretty much cold turkey. 'Cept for the pills. Six years sober now. I even jog to exercise my heart. He sat back in his chair and grinned at Pam. *So that's my whole goddamn sad life story. What about you?*

I married an orthodontist. He drives a Mercedes. He has a very successful practice. We have a daughter. She's a teacher.

Well, holy shit. Good for you. You did all right then. And your parents? They still living in High Park?

Yes, in the same house.

Hey, you're pretty lucky then. I lost both parents. But shit, it's really hard. Your dad was something else, eh? We was all afraid of him. Thought he had goddamn machine guns or something in the basement.

HIGH PARK

William crossed the room and embraced Stella. *Come on, let's you and I take Tanner to the park.* After all these years it was a relief to discuss things openly. To share Tanner with her.

Tanner knew how to pedal along the pathways through the trees. He was happy to be there with his dad. He cycled joyfully along, checking every now and then to make sure William was still behind him. The streamers on his handlebars tossed merrily in the breeze.

William felt content being together with his small son and his grown-up daughter this way. Such moments were rare in his experience, and life had taught him to savour them. *Come*, he said to Stella, pulling on her arm, *let's race him!* Tanner giggled and whooped as his daddy and sister ran past. He pumped his legs energetically, furiously pushing himself to catch up. It was a huge effort. Then they stopped and waited for him. His sister was laughing and his daddy was hugging her.

On the way back to the house, Stella carried the tricycle while William carried the tired little cyclist. He'd worn himself out and was now almost asleep in his father's arms. Stella felt an unexpected wave of affection for the small, beautiful child. *I'm glad you're so happy, Dad.*

Thank you. But you know, Stella, we have to make our happiness in life.

I guess I just haven't quite figured out how yet.

William was silent for a moment. *Fatima is sick. We didn't know. She's going in for surgery next week. They're taking both breasts. I'll be off work for a month. Nothing is for sure.*

God, I'm so sorry.

We just found out. Two weeks ago. It was pretty advanced already.

Can I do anything?

Maybe later. Maybe you could help out with Tanner. I haven't told your grandparents yet. I don't know when to do that. But they'll have to know. I won't be able to come for a while.

Stella looked at her father carefully. His face was flushed, his brow creased. She should have known he was troubled.

GOSSIP

That night Stan took one of his new sleeping pills and went to bed right after dinner. Maria had been fussing over him and might not sleep well herself. So Stella elected to stay over, calling Pam to say only that her grandmother needed some extra companionship. They watched TV together before Maria soon decided that it was time for bed. Stella tidied up in the kitchen and then chatted with Tara—she didn't want to talk about what had happened, but felt she could use some companionship herself.

Hey, you know what? Tara said suddenly.

What?

I saw your mom today. I was just leaving the post office and she was talking to some guy in front of the hardware.

Really? Who was he?

I dunno. Some old guy in a tracksuit. About her age. Never saw him before.

SUNDAY

When Stella arrived home the next morning her mother was already dressed. She'd even put her hair up.

Pam looked at her smugly. *I made bran muffins. Would you like one for breakfast?*

You baked?

Yes! I baked! Don't look at me like that's such a miracle or something.

Well, you haven't baked in a while, Mom. You must be feeling good.

Yes, as a matter of fact I am. I think some tea would be nice.

Stella automatically headed to the kettle. *Sit down, Stella. I'll make it. You've just driven home.*

Stella sat down. She kept looking at her mother, waiting to for the bomb to drop, the complaints to begin. *Are you sure you're okay?*

Of course I am. Why do you keep asking? Stupid girl. Don't I look okay?

You look great, actually. Those pants look good on you. Pam was wearing a form-fitting pair of black slacks that Stella hadn't seen her in for years. She also had on low black heels and a green sweater that highlighted her eyes. *I always liked that sweater on you.*

Pam sashayed past Stella and ran her hand over the seat of the pants. *You don't think they're too tight?*

Uh, no. Stella was struggling to understand what was happening. It was as if she'd fallen into some parallel universe where a woman who looked like her mother had taken over the kitchen. Pam served Stella a cup of tea.

A DRIVE WITH TONY

Over the years Pam had fantasized about meeting him again. Seducing him. Giving him the best sex of his life. But now that he was parked in her driveway in a giant black truck, she didn't know what to do. At the restaurant she'd let on she was happily married. Then, just as they were leaving, she'd somehow admitted she was divorced. Tony's face had lit up with that stupid grin of his.

Then hey, he'd said, *we still got some talkin' to do. You could tell me about it and about your daughter. How about we go somewhere tomorrow? I'll follow you home so I know where you live, and then on Sunday I'll come pick you up and we can take a drive.*

As Pam walked towards Tony's truck he jumped out to open the door for her, just as before. She wondered if Stella was watching from inside the house. She smiled a little to herself. She had certainly surprised her today. Tony showed her where to put her foot on a chrome step and Pam got in. *Where shall we go?*

I dunno; maybe just drive. I can talk good when I'm driving. Is that okay with you?

A drive would be nice.

They drove northwest through the country, past wooded hills and farms and small villages. Every now and then a vista would open up and they could glimpse the mountain and the bay in the distance. *Do you know where we're going?* asked Pam.

I thought Georgian Bay, maybe. There's places we could eat if we wanted to. Sound all right?

She nodded. *I haven't been there in years.*

So how come you and your husband aren't together anymore?

We divorced five years ago, Pam began. *My husband developed other interests. He fell in love with a younger woman. She's an expert in Persian carpets, and he collects them. They have a son together. But he still visits my parents and daughter.*

Well, shit. What was wrong with his eyes? Was he blind or something? Didn't he see what a beautiful woman he was leaving?

Pam laughed self-consciously. *You're still a big flirt, Tony Dinapoli.*

Tony looked at her sideways and smiled. *I just tells it the way I sees it.*

They stopped for coffee at a little place near the pier. Tony was good company, and Pam found him surprisingly easy to talk to. Afterwards they walked to the pier and looked at the historical plaques on ship-building and shipping routes. Pam read the plaques carefully so that she could tell Stella about them when she got home. Tony just looked at the pictures, read a few lines, and darted off to the next sign. Pam didn't even try to keep up with him. She wasn't embarrassed to be seen with him today; he was wearing khaki pants and a striped dress shirt. He still had on his ridiculous running shoes, but the rest of him looked nice.

The wind from the lake was cold and Pam was starting to feel chilly. Tony noticed, and jogged back to his truck to get a blanket. He stood behind her to wrap it around her shoulders and then gently placed his arms around her waist. Pam leaned back against him, closing her eyes. It had been a long time since someone had held her that way.

IMPERFECTION

Stella's father had taught her that the weavers of carpets always included a tiny, almost indiscernible flaw. An intentional mistake. He would study the rugs in his collection, searching for the threads that had been misplaced: The tip of a leaf, the petal of a flower, the end of a tendril. Something minuscule and delicate but clearly imperfect, hidden in the riot of colour and richness, buried in the pattern but locked in. Placed carefully for the eyes of the seeker. Essential to the integrity of the finished product. How strangely like life, she thought, to hide the tiny imperfections, to obscure the blemish. To carry with you the knowledge that what you'd done was less than what it could be. Stella wasn't quite sure what had brought this to mind. Secrets, maybe. Hidden things.

BLOOD SISTERS

Tara and Stella had known each other all their lives. Their mothers had once been good friends but their friendship had waned once the girls finished school. Stella went to university and Tara landed a job with the post office in town. It was a good job, it was unionized, and it suited her personality. She took the odd continuing education course at York University but wasn't particularly serious about finishing a degree. She assumed she'd do what most of their friends did: work until she was married and then settle down in Waldham and have a couple of kids. Tara had been a competitive figure skater and still practiced regularly. She coached at the local arena on Wednesday nights and Sundays, and although the skating moms often drove her crazy, she loved working with the little girls.

Tara was one of the few people in the world whom Stella felt she could be completely honest with. Years ago they'd cut their palms and rubbed them together in a ritual they believed made them blood sisters. No matter where Stella was in the city or what she was doing, she could look down at her hand, find the tiniest little scar, and know that Tara would always be there for her.

STRANGE ELATION

Pam didn't get home till close to eleven that night. They'd stopped in a small town for dinner and then somewhere else for coffee. Tony had been entirely charming. Pam was tired but felt strangely elated. She found the grown-up version of Tony as attractive as she had the adolescent. There was something about his vitality and self-assurance that was still alluring.

Tony helped her step out of the truck and then walked her to the front steps. She debated inviting him in for a nightcap, but Stella would be home and likely still awake. *Thank you for a lovely day, Tony.* Pam extended her hand for a handshake.

What, you kidding me? He pulled her towards him and kissed her on the mouth, inserting his tongue between her teeth and pressing up against her. She stepped back, surprised and knocked off balance. *I may be old*, he grinned, *but I sure as hell ain't dead*.

Pam laughed and he looked instantly wounded.

What? What you laughin' at?

At you. I'm laughing at you. Pam reached out and patted his forearm. *You make me laugh, Tony.*

He looked unconvinced. *So, you wanna see me again? Spend some time together?*

Pam nodded. *Yes. I guess so. Why not?*

Then I'm gonna pick you up on Wednesday at noon. Maybe we'll go to the zoo or something.

Pam nodded again and smiled. As she turned to go Tony smacked her firmly on the butt. She looked around at him, surprised.

You still gotta nice ass, Pam.

The Invalid

Stella was curious. The man who'd come and picked up Pam was, she assumed, the same man Tara had seen her with the week before. Tara's job at the post office generally let her know who was moving into town and who was moving out. She prided herself on keeping track of such things. But when Stella called her after Pam left, they couldn't figure out who he might be.

She smelled a roast cooking when she got home from school that Monday. Her mother had set the table and was busy scraping carrots.

Hi Stella, how was your day?

Mom?

What?

What's going on? You're cooking dinner?

Stella, why do you have to make such a federal case about everything? I'm cooking a roast. Big deal.

Pam put the carrots in a pot and turned on the burner. *You know, I went for a nice drive yesterday.*

Yes, I was meaning to ask you about that.

We drove to Georgian Bay and I saw all these signs about the ship-building industry that used to be there. I think you'd find it interesting. You should go with Tara sometime. She paused. *We went for dinner, too.*

Who is this guy, Mom?

Someone I knew from the old neighbourhood, a long time ago. His wife died. He's living here with his son.

Are you going to see him again?

That's none of your business, Stella. I'm a grown woman. I can do what I want.

Of course.

He's a nice man, that's all. He makes me laugh.

Really?

Why are you surprised? I laugh sometimes. Honestly, Stella, you treat me like I'm an invalid or something.

PAM'S DATE

Pam was waiting by the window long before noon. She'd changed her outfit several times. First she had on a really tight dress, but it made her look fat and so she changed back into her slacks, but then she remembered Tony smacking her on the butt and worried he might think she wanted him to do that again, so she put on a silk shirt dress, one she hadn't worn for some years. It was a little shorter than she liked to wear these days, but her legs were still in good shape and she thought it was particularly flattering. She spent five minutes trying to decide how far down to leave the buttons undone at the neckline. She didn't want to look slutty but she *was* willing to be a little provocative. She decided on four open buttons and an extra spurt of perfume in her cleavage.

When Tony's truck pulled in she stepped back from the window. She wouldn't go rushing out to meet him like a silly schoolgirl. The doorbell rang and she walked to the door slowly, breathing deeply, trying to calm herself. She opened it to see him standing there with a gigantic bouquet. He held it up to her. *Frankie said I should bring you some flowers, so I thought what the hell and bought the biggest bunch they had. I didn't know what you liked.* He grinned his lopsided grin and walked inside. Pam tried to hide her embarrassment, surprise, and pleasure.

So, did I do good?

These are very nice. She'd turned and was heading to the kitchen. *Let me find some vases.*

Tony kicked his shoes off and then bounded along the hall behind her. *Nice place, Pam. Very classy.*

Thank you. I redecorated when William left.

That's good. Something new. Get rid of bad memories. That's what I did, too. Sold the house when Rita died. Bought myself a trailer. Lived in that for a couple of years till I figured out what I wanted. Drove Frankie nuts. Finally I bought another place. But it never felt good. Not like a home, you know. Now I'm living with Frankie. I just parked the thing in his driveway. He don't like it but what the hell. He bought himself one of them townhouses his company is building. It's very "chique." Do you know what "chique" is? That's what he tells me it is. Goddamned "chique."

Pam was arranging the flowers: irises, daisies, gerbera, chrysanthemums, carnations, baby's breath, lilies. She colour-sorted the stems to make different arrangements in four vases. *These must have cost a fortune.*

Tony patted her on the bottom. *As long as you like it, who cares? Those look nice.* He pointed at the arrangements. *So does this.* He patted her bottom again.

Pam blushed. *Tony, stop.*

What? I'm just saying.

Let me place these first, and then we can go. Pam picked up two of the arrangements and Tony grabbed the other two. He followed her through the house while she centred them on tables. *They look so pretty. Thank you.*

Tony was already at the door putting on his shoes. *Hey, Pam, I have an idea. Instead of the zoo, how about mini-golf? I know a place. They got a go-cart track too.*

Pam hesitated. *In this dress?*

Yeah, sure. If it gets in the way, you can just bunch it up or something.

I've never played mini-golf.

I'll teach you. It's fun. C'mon. Let's live a little.

MINI-GOLF

Mini-golf *was* fun, Pam had to admit. Tony was ridiculously good at it and as pleased as anyone could be whenever he or she sank a ball. He was competitive, too, even when playing against a beginner. He knelt on the green when he had a difficult shot; he jumped up and down on the turf trying to make the ball fall in when it was close; he bounded from one part of the course to the next, a forty-five-year-old kid who knew how to thoroughly enjoy himself.

Not that he didn't occasionally put the moves on her. He'd stand behind her with his arms on hers and help her line up a shot, guiding the golf club, pushing his groin up against her backside. He was completely unpredictable; everything he did was unexpected. She found it tiring and amusing and invigorating. And when Tony finished congratulating himself for winning, he suggested trying the go-carts.

Have you never been in one?

No. And I'm not sure I want to try.

C'mon, Pam, we're having a good time, ain't we? Trust me. It's something you gotta do at least once in your life.

Why don't you do it and I'll watch.

No way. You're coming too. Tony took her hand and dragged her to the starter line. *Wait here and I'll get our tickets.*

Tony waved at the young attendant and pointed at Pam. *Hey, kid, we need a couple of helmets here.*

What about my hair?

Comb it later. Don't worry. Tony strode off towards the booth and was back quickly with a strip of tickets. He helped Pam adjust her helmet and climb into the cart. He showed her the accelerator and brake. *You know how to drive,* he said. *It's the same thing. Just floor it. Nothing can happen. I'll give you a head start.*

Pam was nervous, but didn't want to look it. She was ready to stop being cautious and careful. This was an unexpected chance to have some fun, and something she could think about after Tony moved on again. The attendant did something with a rope at the back of her car and she felt the engine starting. She couldn't blow it by being a spoilsport. So she tucked her dress between her knees, put her foot to the floor, and jerked forward with a tremendous burst of power. She drove right into a wall of tires.

Turn your wheel and gas it! Tony shouted.

Pam turned her wheel and floored the accelerator. She took off at high speed and found herself leaning into a curve, making her first big turn. She smiled broadly. She was doing it. Tony whizzed pass her yelling something she couldn't make out. She went faster but couldn't keep up. He was a speed demon. She continued driving the course as quickly as she dared, trying not to humiliate herself by hitting the tires again. Tony lapped her, screaming.

When she finished the course, the attendant helped her out of the cart and took her helmet. Her legs felt wobbly. Tony was waiting for her. *You did good. You're a natural.* He grinned. *I told you it was fun.* He slung his arm around her shoulders and walked her to his truck. *Hey, Pam,* he said, opening her door, *I'm having a hell of a good time.*

Pam got in and put her hands to her cheeks. She was afraid she was blushing. She patted her hair. *I must look a sight.*

Tony pulled his door shut. *What you look like is someone who's having a good time with a very charming guy.*

Pam laughed at him. She laughed because he didn't care how her hair looked and she laughed because he was easy to be with and she was having fun. She laughed because she hadn't laughed so openly with anyone else for a long time. William had always been so serious. Stella, too. And her parents. Everyone was always intense or worried or uptight. This was what she'd been missing all those years, she thought. Someone to laugh with.

Tony was watching her. *What's going on in there?* He pointed to her temple.

I was just thinking how pleasant it is to be with you.

That's good, Pam. Really good.

Did you take your wife go-carting?

Rita? No. But I took Frankie. Every summer as soon as the track opened. Two or three times a week we went.

What was she like?

Tony turned on the truck and rested his hands on the steering wheel. *She was like this ball of light.* He made a globe shape with his hands. *She came into a room and it just got brighter and better. Everybody loved her. She was a great mother. Frankie adored her. But you know, then she was gone. Just like that. We didn't know what the hell to do with ourselves.*

Pam nodded.

So the thing is, you know, when you lose someone like that, you finally say "What the hell, I'm gonna live a little, enjoy what time I got. Not gonna put anything off."

Tony looked at Pam. His eyes were damp and he wiped away a tear that had escaped. *So that's my sad story.*

PAM'S CONSCIENCE

Pam hadn't allowed herself to dwell on her past history with Tony. She enjoyed his company but wasn't really expecting him to stick around. He'd left her once, after all. And William had left too. There was no reason to believe this would be a long-term thing. He'd obviously loved his wife a great deal. She could never favourably compare with the memory of a woman he described as a *ball of light*.

But if he did stick around, Pam wondered, how could she introduce him to Stella? Did he remember enough to figure it out? Would he ask himself if Stella was his? Pam decided that she'd simply take two years off Stella's age. That way Tony would never think to question. Stella wouldn't be any the wiser, and no one would be hurt. Pam's conscience bothered her a little, but why upset things?

HEART ATTACK

Stella had been marking for hours when the house phone rang. This didn't happen often. She paused in her work and listened for her mother to pick up the phone. A telemarketer, probably, or some sort of phone survey. Someone selling tickets to the circus. *Oh God,* she heard Pam saying, panic in her voice. *Oh, God.* Throwing down her pen, Stella rushed down the stairs. *What is it? What's wrong?*

Your grandfather, said Pam, holding the phone to her chest. *He had a heart attack and he's in the hospital. Your grandmother is calling. She wants me to call your father.*

Here, said Stella, taking the phone. *Grandma? Are you okay? Where are you? Can you stay there until I come? Yes. Yes, I'll call Dad. See you soon.*

Stella reached for a jacket out of the closet. Picking up her purse and keys from the hall table, she leaned over to kiss her mother. *Go to bed, I'll look after things. Don't worry. Dad will be there. I'll spend the night with Grandma.*

I don't like you driving at night, Stella. Why not go in the morning?

Without answering, Stella swung open the front door and rushed outside, pulling her phone out as she went. *Dad, Grandpa's in emergency at St. Joseph's.*

Stella sped south to the hospital. Once she arrived she had to drive through several tiers of the parking lot before finding a spot. Then, walking quickly, she navigated the hallways, following the signs to the emergency department. Her father was there before her, getting directions from the nurse at the station. Stella saw his broad shoulders encased in the familiar navy trench coat: Aquascutum, classic and timeless.

As Stella rushed towards him he reached out his left arm in a half embrace and then guided her down the hall to a curtained enclosure. A curled figure lay under a thin yellow sheet. Her grandmother sat in a plastic chair by the foot of the bed watching anxiously while the nurse checked and adjusted settings on the clear tubes curling around and under the mounded sheet.

Maria looked frail, jaundiced in the fluorescent lighting, her mismatched cardigan and patterned dress shabby and out of place. As a black machine produced a wobbly thin green line she stared fixedly at the screen.

Maria, said her father quietly, placing his hand on her shoulder. *Maria, are you all right?* She shook her head and pointed feebly at the green line.

It was a heart attack. Very serious. We will not know for seventy-two hours how much is the damage. "Your husband had a heart attack," *the ambulance man said.* "Who can we call?" *I opened my purse and gave my little book, and he called Pam. That's it.*

It will be all right, said William. *The doctors deal with these all the time. I'm sure they have lots of drugs that will help Stan to stabilize. Let me go find someone to talk to.*

Stella reached for her grandmother's hand and clasped it tightly, trying to infuse the cold fingers with strength and courage. She couldn't see Stan's face; he was turned to the wall, and by the sound of his breathing, appeared to be sleeping. Every minute or so a watery-raspy intake of breath would sound. She could feel her grandmother stiffen in the long seconds between each one.

Soon William came back and signalled Stella to join him in the hallway. *It's bad. The doctors believe there's a lot of damage. It was several minutes before the ambulance arrived. He was without oxygen for a long time. It's not clear whether he'll pull through.*

My God, how do you explain this to Pam? Stella thought of her mother alone at home, tucked into bed, the night light left on in the bathroom. She began to panic and felt her breath leaving her, a sharp, piercing ice thrusting down deep into her chest. She closed her eyes and began to sway. Her father grabbed her. *Stella, bear up. We have to go to Maria. We have to stay with her, support her. This will be hardest on her.*

Stella felt her father's hands on her shoulders and opened her eyes. *Of course, Dad.* The thought of Pam had not yet come to him. His concern was only for her grandmother. Together they walked back into the room.

THE KADDISH

Stella looked back at the monitor. The green line continued to trace out the remaining moments of her grandfather's existence. Little spikes and dips, long flat stretches, very tiny spikes, indiscernible dips, flat stretches. Maria's eyes catalogued every movement, followed the markings. The raspy breaths had a gurgle to them, a desperate wet gurgle-rattle.

Tell me, said Maria, her gaze not leaving the monitor, her words directed at William. *Tell me what they told you.*

And Stella marvelled at her father, marvelled that he, not wavering, went to her grandmother and knelt before her, and taking both hands in his, said, *We must prepare for the worst.*

Stella stood by silently waiting for a reaction, an outburst. Instead Maria lowered her head, dropping her gaze for the first time. And then she stood. She went to her husband's side. She kissed his hands and face and stroked his cheek ever so gently. Then she began to hum, sounding a plaintive rhythm that came from deep inside. Unbidden music. Placing her hands over her husband's, with her eyes closed she began to rock, still humming, and then intoned words Stella didn't understand. She and her father stood in silence.

Hear O Israel, the Lord is our God, the Lord is one, said her grandmother, reverting to English. *He will rest now.* She nodded at William and walked towards him. He opened his arms and embraced her gently. The three of them stood together while the rasping breaths became rapidly louder and more laboured. Suddenly the monitor began to beep an alarm. Two nurses and a doctor came in. They checked the monitor and calmly placed the stethoscope on Grandfather Lipinski's chest. Respectfully, they lifted his wrist. There was no pulse, and there was no breath left. They softly turned off the machine and left them in the blessed stillness.

AFTERMATH

After a long silence, William was the first to speak. *Maria, let me drive you home. Stella will stay with you.* Tenderly, he took Maria's hand and guided her from the curtained room, out of the unit, and through to the reception area.

Stay here, he told Stella, *while I get the car.*

Together they led Maria out to the car and into her seat. No one spoke. William drove quickly and with the assurance of a man in charge. He pulled into the driveway and shut off the ignition.

You stay here, he said again to Stella. *I'll be back in the morning. I'll bring Pam. Then we'll get your car.* Walking them to the door of the house, William squeezed Stella's arm and kissed Maria's forehead. Suddenly brittle from her trauma, Maria seemed to break. She fell into him abruptly, sobbing, her stooped body racked by her grief. William held her upright, biting his bottom lip, clenching his eyes closed. The sadness of her loss infusing him with the fresh pain of his own grief, he wept silently while holding her.

Stella stood quietly aside. Finally, she slipped her hand under her grandmother's arm and led her slowly up the stairs to the house. At each step she waited for Maria to bend her knee and shift her weight so that she could propel herself upwards. They shuffled directly to the bedroom. Stella turned on the light and drew down the covers. Her grandmother sat down heavily and waited for Stella to unlace and remove her shoes. Stella did so quickly, expertly, and then helped her grandmother lie down and tucked her in. Then she lay down beside her and held her hand until she saw that she slept.

She sat on a chair in the room throughout the night. Once, when she got up to straighten the coverlet, she saw that her grandmother's face was entirely wet. She'd been weeping, noiselessly, in her sleep.

Stella's own grief she left unexamined. There was too much to do. She knew that when Pam arrived there would be many questions and many jobs. At one point in the night, Stella found a pen in her bag and a used envelope. *Funeral arrangements,* she wrote. Then, under that: *Service. Flowers. Food. Newspaper announcement. Funeral home. Coffin. Burial plot. Tombstone.* How does one arrange these things, Stella wondered. Where does one begin?

At nine o'clock she rose and left her sleeping grandmother to make tea and toast. She loaded a dingy metal tray embossed with tulips and carried it down the hall. *Gran, you might want to get up now. It's morning.*

Maria looked at Stella, at the room, at her own clothed body. *It was not a bad dream?*

No, Gran. I'm sorry. It's all true. I've brought you some tea.

Nodding softly, her grandmother sat up and reached for the tea cup. *Thank you, luby.* Her words were so faint that Stella could scarcely hear her.

Dad will be here soon.

With your mother, said Maria, shaking her head. *She will have something to say.*

Yes, I'm sure she will.

Stella waited until Maria had finished the tea, and then handed her the tray with the toast and half a grapefruit. *You need to eat, Gran.*

She took the tray compliantly and smiled weakly at Stella in appreciation. Then the alarm chime sounded and the side door slammed shut. *That will be Mom*, Stella said, leaving the room.

Where's Ma? snapped Pam, coming down the hall. *I have to see her.*

In the bedroom, eating breakfast. Shall I make you something? Her mother pushed past her and hurried down the hall. Stella waited. Soon she heard Pam crying and shrieking and then her grandmother's voice soothing her.

William stood in the kitchen. *Did she sleep?*

Yes, a little. I made her some breakfast.

Your mother is upset, and she was angry that you didn't call her.

I'm sorry. I was so busy looking after Gran.

Maybe apologize later?

She came with you, though. She didn't mind?

William smiled. *Oh, she minded. Sat in the back seat. Said she couldn't stand to be near me.*

I'm sorry.

It's nothing to do with you.

Want some tea?

Tea would be good.

Stella poured her father·a cup and sat down with him at the little grey Formica table. Plastic geraniums had been placed in a dollar-store bud vase in the centre. The splash of colour delighted Stella. It was cheerful. Pam, though, would be disgusted by its cheapness. It would not at all please Pam.

We have a lot to do, Dad. I started a list.

Good, let me see it. He reached for the envelope and scanned the list. *This will be expensive, Stella. Funerals cost money. I'll pay.*

Are you sure, Dad? Will Mom let you?

I expect so, he said, smiling at her.

Have you told Tanner?

No, not yet. Tonight maybe, when I go home.

I guess it will be hard to explain.

Yes, it will be very hard. Something in his voice caught. Stella looked up at him. There were tears on his cheeks, and he was swiping at them with the sleeve of his shirt.

Dad?

I loved your grandfather very much, Stella. This is a sad time for us all.

Stella sat there stonily, unmoving. She needed to take her own grief and hold it next to her heart until she could let it blaze in privacy, away from the others. In the park maybe, by the cherry trees where she'd had such happy times with her grandfather, but not here. Not when the needs of others were intruding so heavily.

Pam entered the kitchen. *Ma is washing and changing. We have to make the arrangements. Have you called anyone?*

Not yet, but Stella has started a list. We begin with the funeral home and the church, I think.

And who asked you? Pam said. *Why are you still here anyway? You think I need you to do this for my own father?*

Mom! Dad has offered to help, and to pay for everything.

Who else should pay? I don't have money for this and I'm sure they don't either. Unless it's in a jam jar somewhere in the basement.

Mom, can you not try to be nice? I want Dad here and I'm pretty sure that if you asked Grandma she'd say the same thing.

William stood. *Stella,* he said softly, *why don't I drive you to the hospital to pick up your car. While we're gone, your mother can decide if she wants my help. I'll wait outside.* Stiffly, proudly, William left the kitchen.

Stella looked at her mother with some disgust. *I better go. Try to be nice to Gran while I'm gone.*

William was waiting in the car. *I'm sorry, Stella, your mother and I don't do very well together.*

I know, don't worry.

They drove in silence for a few minutes. *Dad, what was that prayer that Grandma sang last night? It didn't sound like Polish.*

No, it did not. I believe it was Hebrew.

Where would she have learned that?

Well, I don't know. It may be one of those things that reveal themselves after a time.

Should we ask her about it?

No, I don't think so. She'll tell us if we need to know and when she's ready.

It doesn't make sense.

War makes people do desperate stuff, Stella. Things are not always what they seem.

It was a puzzling comment. She would save it, and explore its meaning when she could.

Your mother will be having a very hard time with this. Despite how she acts or what she might say. This will be scary for her. It signals the beginning of another stage in life, and new stages are stressful and frightening at first.

Stella looked out the window and studied a passing streetcar. *Do you mean like the time when you left and started a new family?*

William took that in. *In part. I think there are phases in our lives, and that as we pass from one to the other we leave things behind. It's sad and very often painful. We leave people behind too, and not always on purpose. I think that's what both Maria and your mother are going to have to deal with. What will their new world look like? We need to be patient with them and kind.*

I don't know how to deal with her some days. She's in a lot of pain sometimes and at other times she seems more than fine. We seldom have just normal conversations.

I'm deeply sorry you're dealing with this. Your mother has chosen to live a certain way. But now is not the time for change. Now is the time for us to be understanding.

Thanks, Dad.

William reached over and squeezed Stella's arm.

THE MASS

The funeral mass was held at St. Casimir's. Three-cornered sandwiches and coffee and squares were served in the parish hall afterwards. William had found a florist who had accessed fresh poppies. Amid a wide spray of fern they covered the casket and featured in several of the free-standing arrangements. Maria was much moved by William's gesture, and had broken down and sobbed. *How did you know?* she asked him. *How did you know that Stan gave me poppies when we were married?* Pam told Stella that she would have preferred roses, but no one had asked her.

Stella was surprised at the number of people there—friends from the neighbourhood, some of her father's colleagues, and even some people from her school. This completely took her aback. She'd called in her absence, but it hadn't occurred to her that others might think it important to acknowledge her loss. She was grabbed up and hugged by Tara and Tara's parents and a clutch of fellow teachers from Waldham. The student council had sent flowers. This floored her. She was overwhelmed by her two worlds' sudden collision and didn't know how to respond.

William's wife and son attended the mass but sat discreetly in a back pew on their own. Stella approached Fatima after the service and introduced herself. Tanner smiled and let her give him a hug before rushing off down the aisle towards his father. Fatima had dressed in black and was wearing a lace scarf draped loosely over her hair and shoulders. She held Stella's hand for a long moment and said how sorry she was for her loss but how glad she was to finally meet her. Stella was nervous and had to try really hard not to stare at Fatima's chest, heavily bandaged under her dress. Pam might be nearby and she was worried she'd make a scene. Stella thanked Fatima for coming and quickly excused herself.

She went in search of Pam, finally spotting her standing in a quiet corner of the hall talking to man in a dark suit. He had thick greying hair and kept taking half steps forward and then back as though it was impossible for him to stand in one place. Stella paused and watched them for a moment. *Could this be her mother's new old friend?*

Tara appeared at her side. *Who's your mother with?*

I dunno. I've never seen him before. Have you?

Maybe. He looks a little like Tracksuit Guy, but I'm not sure.

That's what I'm thinking.

Why don't you go meet him?

No. I better not. If she wanted me to meet him she'd introduce us.

The man in the navy suit scanned the room indifferently until his gaze fell upon Stella and Tara.

He's staring at you.

He is not.

He is. And now your mother's looking too. We better go over.

Stella and Tara linked arms and approached Pam.

Hi, Mom.

Mrs. Wheeler, I'm so sorry for your loss. Tara kissed Pam on the cheek.

Thank you, Tara. The flowers your family sent are beautiful. It was very kind. I'm touched that all of you came.

Stella looked at the man pointedly and raised her eyebrows slightly.

This is Mr. Dinapoli. He's a friend of mine. He knew your grandfather, Stella.

Stella reached out to shake his hand. *Thank you for coming.*

The man grasped Stella's hand and held on to it for a little longer than necessary. *I'm very sorry for your loss.*

Thank you. There was something vaguely familiar about him, thought Stella. She must have met him before somewhere.

Mr. Dinapoli continued to stare at her. He looked at Pam quickly and then looked back at Stella. His look was penetrating; he was clearly studying her. *You look like your mother,* he said finally.

Well that was weird, said Tara as they walked away. *He was kind of intense. But he looks familiar. Like I've seen him somewhere, and not just in his tracksuit.*

SITTING SHIVA

That night at the house on Indian Grove, a strange occurrence took place. After sundown and a light meal, the doorbell began to ring and friends of her grandparents, along with neighbours and local shop owners, filed into the living room. They sat down quietly along its walls, and although most had brought food, they refused any offers of tea and coffee. Maria didn't seem surprised to see them. That's when Stella, from her perch in the kitchen, noticed for the first time that all the sheets had been removed from the furniture. A black cloth draped the hall mirror and someone had stopped the wooden cuckoo clock in the dining room. After Maria had greeted everyone and they were all seated, Stella watched as she went to join her guests. But then, before taking her seat on a low footstool, she grabbed hold of her dress and made a small rip near her left breast.

Stella turned to William with a quizzical look. *They're sitting Shiva,* he explained. *Your grandmother is observing the old ways as well as the new.*

I don't understand. We just had Mass.

You're crazy! snapped Pam. *She's doing no such thing. They're not bloody Jews.*

William nodded in the direction of the living room. The three of them peered around the corner of the kitchen. An older man wearing a yarmulke and a prayer shawl stood at one end of the room reciting something in Hebrew, followed by English.

Glorified and sanctified be God's great name . . .

We should join them, said William, *and show respect.* He walked quietly into the living room and took a seat on the floor. Maria nodded at him and smiled.

I don't bloody believe this, said Pam. *What is he doing? What the hell are they doing?*

I don't know, Mom, but it's obviously important. Maybe we should go in.

No goddamn way, Pam hissed. *Haven't I had enough to deal with? Take me home. I'm not going to stay here another minute.*

Mom, think of Grandma. She'll be upset if we leave.

I don't care, Stella. Take me home. Or if you won't do it, I'll ask somebody else.

She swept out of the house in a cloud of indignation. Stella followed her outside, where Pam continued to rail against stupid people, stupid friends, and secrets. *How could they keep this from me?* was a recurring question in her litany of outrage. *What does this make me? A Jewess? What does it make you? A half-Jew? How could they? They'll rot in purgatory. They can't be buried in consecrated ground. They took communion, for God's sake!*

INDIAN GROVE

Stella returned to the house only after the cab she'd called finally arrived to collect Pam. By that time the guests were beginning to leave, paying their respects to Maria before they did. *May God comfort you,* each intoned, clasping her grandmother's hands and speaking solemnly. They repeated the gesture with both William and Stella before stepping out into the night.

Her grandmother looked sad and exhausted. *How is Pamela?*

Mom is fine, don't worry about her.

She did not expect us to sit Shiva, I think.

No, Gran, that was a bit of a surprise.

For all of us, added William.

It was for the best, said Maria. *There is no easy way to explain.*

Stella helped her grandmother get ready for bed and returned to find William drinking schnapps in the kitchen. He held up his glass. *To Stan, may he rest in peace.*

Stella sat across from him and put her face in her hands. *Now what?*

Now we do everything we can to support your grandmother, and then we begin to look after the other people in our lives whom we love.

I met Fatima today. She's lovely.

I'm glad you think so. I always hoped you two would get along.

Does Tanner understand that his grandpa is gone?

I don't know how you explain that to a child. He'll visit the house and miss him, and eventually he'll get used to missing him, and then perhaps he will forget.

Grandpa really loved him, I could tell.

Yes. It was mutual.

THE PARK

William didn't head home until two o'clock in the morning. As he drove, he found himself thinking about the park that had played such a big part in the shaping of his life. As a young man he would often study there in the late afternoons. Sometimes he'd just walk around and watch the ducks and the geese, and at other times he'd gaze at the couples walking hand in hand and wonder about their happiness.

He loved the park in the crisp autumn when brittle leaves littered the pathways, in the spring when the grass turned a vibrant green and the blossoms opened, in the lazy summer when families played and had picnics in the shade, and mostly in the winter when the park grew hushed with the snow and you could read the tracks to see which animals had crossed the fields and how many fellow travellers had walked where you were walking. The park was where he'd strolled with Stan and discussed the affairs of the world, and it was where they took Tanner to ride his tricycle. It was his special place. But it had also been his undoing.

One summer evening he'd seen Pam there with a group of boys. It worried him. He stood under the shadow of a tree as two of the boys wandered off, leaving Pam alone with a tall, dark-haired boy. There was awkward embracing and awkward groping, then they lay down together under a lilac bush. William didn't want to be a voyeur. But Pam was vulnerable. He waited until she rose and straightened her dress and then he followed slowly after her, ensuring her safe passage through the darkness.

He returned to the park the next evening. Pam was standing by the lilac bush and crying. He waited while she waited. No one appeared. Finally she wiped at her face and moved through the grass back to the street. Again he followed slowly, guarding her.

The next two nights were the same. Pam waited stoically at the lilac bush, nicely dressed, looking brave and hopeful. Gradually her shoulders would drop and she would begin to wipe at her tears. Each night she waited, and each night he shadowed her return home.

When she came to him in his room he knew that her need was desperate and that her passion was not for him. But he took her in his arms, remembering her fallen shoulders. Later, he knew the child wasn't his. But he wanted to safeguard her, and he wanted a family. Stan and Maria mattered to him, Pam mattered to him. The baby that became Stella wasn't the price of admission. She was a wonderful gift.

THE TALK

Tony had called several times since the funeral, but Pam had been short with him. For the next while, she said, she'd be too busy to see him. Pam was dreading the questions he might ask. She'd seen his face when he first saw Stella. And she was fully prepared to lie. How could he ever check Stella's real age? It's not as if he'd walk up to her and ask to see her birth certificate. This was the best way. After all this time, it was the only way. Stella worshipped William. It was the one good and pure thing Pam had done, and she wouldn't take that away from them.

Stella noticed that her mother's moods were once more on the prickly side of things. She wondered what had happened to Mr. Dinapoli. There had been no sign of him since the funeral.

Pam had upped her naturopathic remedies and needed to replenish her supply. She was about to set off for the herbal store one morning when the doorbell rang. Tony stood there in dress pants and a sports coat, rocking back and forth in a pair of polished loafers. She smiled to see that he was without his running shoes.

Can I come in?

I was just going out, actually.

Can it wait? We need to talk.

I'm awfully busy, Tony. I need to go. Her hands were trembling. She knew she was ruining whatever it was they had, but there was no way she'd risk having the truth come out.

Tony walked inside, shut the door firmly behind him, and pulled Pam close. He kissed her gently, lingeringly, on the mouth and then suddenly stepped back. *There. I been meaning to do that. Now tell me what the goddamn hell is going on. You don't want to see me no more?*

Pam was distressed and not a little astonished. She was also aroused. He looked great. His aftershave smelled great. His arms were strong. She could still taste him on her lips.

Pam? You gonna answer me? He looked at her closely. *I think we got some things to talk about.*

Pam was thinking furiously. Should she distract him? Ask him to leave? Make a pot of coffee and lie? It's not like she owed him anything. Mister Here-Today-and-Gone-Tomorrow.

Pam. Tony reached out and cupped her face in his hands. He tipped it up so that she was forced to look at him. *I'm not going anywhere until you talk to me.*

I'll make a pot of coffee.

No. Me and Rita, we did this thing. Our serious talks, even when we were mad, we had in the bedroom. She said it kept things in perspective.

I'm not going into the bedroom with you.

We're going to take off our shoes and lie down on the bed and hold hands and you're going to tell me what's going on. Then later, if something else comes to mind, we'll be in the right place.

I'm not doing that, Tony. We don't even know each other that well.

Pam, you've got to give a little. I can show you. Tony kicked off his loafers and headed down the hall. *Is this it?* he called, standing outside her room.

Pam followed. *What if Stella comes home?*

Shut your door. She's a big girl, right? What is she, maybe twenty-five now?

No! Twenty-three. She's only twenty-three.

Tony looked at her sharply. *You sure about that? I was guessing twenty-five.* He lay down on Pam's bed and patted the space beside him. Then he crossed his ankles comfortably and put his hands behind his head. *See, Rita said this was the only way she could keep me in one place long enough to have a serious conversation.* He grinned.

Pam locked her door and closed the curtains. He wouldn't be able to see her face. She could do this. She just had to stick to her story. She lay down on the edge of the bed, as far from Tony as she could manage without falling off. Tony reached for her hand and rested it on his chest, clasping his hands on top of it.

Ya know, when I saw your daughter I was shocked. I said to myself, My God, she looks just like my sister Anna. I swear to God, I thought I was looking at Anna when she was young again. And I thought, how is this possible? What kind of coincidence is this?

Well, they say everyone has a double. I saw on TV once where they were talking about it. Apparently everyone shares facial characteristics with other people.

Yeah, you think so?

It's possible.

Tony turned over on his side and looked at Pam seriously. *You know what I been thinking? I been thinking that maybe she's twenty-five and I know who the father is.*

Don't be ridiculous, Tony. Stella is twenty-three. Pam stood up abruptly and paced around the room. *Why would you say such a thing? Stella and her father are close. She's his spit. They do everything together. She's twenty-three and that's the end of it. If you don't believe me you can just leave.* Pam pointed at the doorway. She was genuinely angry now. He had no right to put her in this position.

Tony jumped up, crossed the room, and tried to put his arms around her. She struggled to back away. *Tell me again,* he said tenderly. *Look into my eyes and tell me she's not mine.*

Pam pushed him. *I've told you enough times and I won't say it again. Leave it alone. She loves William. He's her father. The past should stay in the past.*

Tony looked at her and shook his head. *I should go.*

AFTERMATH

Pam stayed in her room until she heard the front door open and close. Tony was gone and she was glad. What right did he have to lay claim to Stella? Had he given any thought to what this might do to the girl? He was a selfish prick who wanted to prove he was virile or something. She'd managed without him this long and could certainly manage again.

Stella wasn't like other girls. She was a deep thinker and she was loyal. You couldn't say to a girl like Stella, *Oh, by the way, I lied to you about your father. It's actually this guy you met at your grandfather's funeral. He knocked me up and I tricked William into marrying me.* It would destroy her world. So nobody, not even Tony Dinapoli, was going to charm the truth out of her.

But when her anger passed, Pam was sad. They'd had fun together. She smiled to think of Rita making him lie down on bed for serious talks. He was always bouncing and darting and jogging off somewhere. That much hadn't changed since they were young. Mister Charming Ants-in-His-Pants.

Pam was forty-one years old. William had been gone for five years. It was a long time for someone her age to be shelved. She felt redundant and unwanted. Divorce did that to you. Being displaced by a younger woman did that to you. Maybe it would have been different if they'd had more children—maybe if she'd given William a son he would have stayed. She'd seen him with that beautiful little boy at the funeral and had guessed he was William's. And the woman dressed in black talking to Stella: that must be the new wife.

She knew she should have approached her and thanked her for coming. But she couldn't do it. She was still too damn mad. Besides, Tony was there distracting her by being sympathetic and thoughtful. He'd even sent a nice arrangement of roses to the funeral home. Unlike the stupid poppy spray William bought. But Ma had loved the poppies. She'd taken one out of the spray and tucked it in her bosom. They obviously meant something to her. William was like that, always figuring things out before she did. It was annoying. And always so damn proper. Why couldn't he just lose his temper once in a while? Put her in her place? Tony wouldn't put up with her shit. He'd made that clear already.

But he was gone now. She had been her worst self and she'd let him go. She couldn't have let him know how frightened she'd been at sixteen, unmarried and pregnant. You can't explain that to a guy like Tony. Easy come, easy go Tony. Not like William. William would think about it, and would understand what she'd had to do. He wouldn't be mad about it, either. He might be disappointed or gently suggest another approach, but he'd never been mad at her. Why had they never laughed together? Deep belly laughs. Had they *ever* lain on the bed together and held hands to talk? She couldn't remember.

PAM AND STELLA

When Stella arrived home there was no sign of her mother. She found her lying on the bed, fully clothed, an ice pack on her forehead.

Headache?

The worst.

Can I get you anything?

Maybe another Tylenol.

How many have you had?

Four today. Six. I'm not sure.

Maybe we should wait a bit. Can I make you something to eat?

No. I don't want anything.

Has something upset you? You've been feeling so well lately.

I don't want to talk about it.

Maybe you should.

No.

What's wrong?

I'm just sad.

About Grandpa?

No. Yes. That too.

What else?

*I just feel old and unwanted. And I'm too young to feel that way.
I don't want to be alone for another thirty or forty years.*

You're not alone. I'm here.

*You won't stay. You'll get married or go travelling with Tara or do
something else. And then it will just be me.*

I won't go far.

*Well, you should. You're smart. Why get stuck here when you can
do other things with your life? You should travel. You should have fun.
You should laugh. Don't end up like me.*

What are you talking about?

*I just don't think we laughed enough. I think that's why your father
went looking for someone else. We never held hands and talked.*

Mom, you're scaring me a bit.

*Listen, I'm forty-one and I'm alone: you don't want to end up
this way.*

MARIA'S STORY

Stella had planned her visit to Indian Grove so that she could
help her grandmother with her Saturday shopping. They'd
just gotten back and Stella was stowing the fresh fruit and vegetables in the fridge while Maria took off her shoes and stretched
her legs.

*Grandma, Grandpa always talked about the war, but I've never
heard your side of things. What was it like, or is it too painful?*

*Ah, luby, you don't know what you ask. These stories hurt. So
much pain and fear. It was a dark time. I don't like to remember.*

*I'm sorry. I just wanted to know more about you, not so much the
bad stuff.*

*It was all bad. The Krauts, the Russkies. They did wicked things
and no one could stop them. God had abandoned the Poles and the Jews
to such suffering.*

Was there nothing good about that time? Nothing worth sharing?

*Stella, it was a bad dream. The Russkies came first, and it was a big
surprise. Our cavalry was strong. Good, brave men and beautiful horses.
But the tanks came and big trucks. They loaded the men on the trucks and*

drove away. The tanks drove across the countryside. You could feel the earth moving under your feet there were so many. We were a proud country but nothing would stop the tanks. And then the Krauts came with their guns. They killed and killed. And we hid in the woods, digging holes under the tree roots on the side of the river. But it was winter and so cold. I hid in my hole with blankets and prayed to die before they found me. We would sneak out when it was quiet and go back to our houses for food, but each time some of the houses were burned and everything ruined. Sometimes you could hear that they were waiting, and they would grab the women and use them for filth. For days I hid in my hole and could hear the screaming. And then one day I realized it was over, the animals had gone. Still the screams and the guns I could hear for many days.

How did you escape?

It was a strange happening. You see, the Russkies came back. And this time it was the Krauts they were after. More tanks came than before. Hundreds of tanks. Dead Krauts lay in the snow everywhere you could see. The Russkies were winning and the Krauts began to retreat. But still we were not safe because the Russian men were pigs. The fighting by Vistula River was the worst. Blood ran in the water. People stopped drinking from the river, afraid they would drink dirty blood. Instead, they melted snow on small fires.

This is a very strange thing, Stella. God abandoned us to evil. But when the Krauts left, then the Russkies started to retreat too. They drove their tanks on the frozen river. A big line. We were happy to see them go. Then some of the tanks fell in. How many, I don't know. Maybe five or six, maybe two dozen. A hot sun came and many tanks got stuck in the earth, and some went into the river, and the Russkies had to climb out and walk to Moscow. It was God finally noticing us.

And then we walked in the opposite direction. The Krauts went to the northeast, and the Russkies went to Moscow, so we walked south. At night. We carried food and blankets. Maybe ten families together. But no men. The men were all prisoners. We stayed together and hid during the day and walked in the night. Then, one day, we were sleeping, huddled in a group, away from the road, when we heard gunfire and trucks. The Krauts found us and tied us together and made us walk behind the truck. Anyone who fell down was shot and left. Who lived, was taken to Theresienstadt.

Oh, Gran. Over the years Stella had heard of the notorious Theresienstadt, a so-called holding camp where the wealthy and distinguished families were treated well and the rest were expected to farm or split mica. Stan had told her that the Nazis had once allowed the Red Cross to inspect the camp, but not before concealing its true conditions. Stella sensed that Maria's time there wasn't something she wanted to remember. She moved closer now and hugged her.

Maria patted her arm gently and continued. *So, the rest of the war was in the camp. Some days it was not so bad. I had friends in my Hundertschaft, the strong labour group. Mostly we did cleaning and farm labouring. We worked hard, long hours with only a little bread and sometimes a piece of cabbage or turnip or potato, not on the same day, but together we speak Polish and encourage each other. The Americans, we thought, would come to save us. In the end it was the Russkies who came. May 8, 1945. We were locked in the barracks. No one had food or latrines that day. No one went to the work. The Czech guards were excited. They stood outside the gates with their guns. Then we saw a jeep coming, and it pulled up to the gates and two Russkies get out and talk to the guards. One of them shouts and says "Open the gates," and the jeep drives into the courtyard and shouts, "Everybody get out!" And we all run to the Russkies and some people picked them up and carried them. It was confusing and very sudden. But the Russkies and the Czechs, they don't want us. They tell us to go. We are free, but we must go.*

Then what? Stella was sitting beside Maria now, holding her hands in her own.

THE RED CROSS

I waited. I stood back and waited to see what was the best. I went to the kitchen and there was no one there, and I took many potatoes. I put them in my blouse and tied it very tight to me. And I went back to my bed and I rested for my journey. There was no one else in the dormitory. I slept. And the next morning, there was many people from the Red Cross and from the British Army and there was your grandfather. Stanislaw found me sleeping and he waked me up and took me to the tent for nursing. I had lice and diphtheria and many sores and a bad cough but I was free. So Stanislaw waited for me and together we followed the Americans and took a troop carrier to the United States. We did not have any papers and it was difficult to find work. And so with other refugees, we came to Canada. And here Stanislaw found work in the linseed oil factory and we stayed.

You were so brave.

Not so brave, luby. I was scared always. You never forget so much fear. It stays with you.

And now?

In the night. I wake up and I have a dream, and I am still in the camp working on the farm, being so hungry. And the men all the time watching, watching and waiting for a chance, any excuse to be cruel. They used sticks and their guns to bash us. They used their filthy hands to do other things. Every day they watched and they laughed together and they treated us like animals. That never goes away, luby.

SHAME

A nd Grandpa? Was he still so scared too?

For men, it was different. Scared, yes. Sure. And ashamed. They are men. They think they can fix everything. There is shame when they see things they cannot fix. When they are powerless. That is what it is to be a man. They carry shame.

Stella thought. *Gran, I remember this story Grandpa told about hiding in a cellar closet in Holland. Is that the sort of thing you mean? He couldn't help that girl without risking his life and so he was ashamed?*

Maria paused before answering. *So many sad things, Stella. Yes, I think your grandfather wanted to help her. But it was not his own life he risked, it was the lives of the men with him, and also the good Dutch people who hid them. One girl to be raped and murdered or a handful of soldiers and a large group of Dutch? He had to choose. But such a choice is hard. You never recover from such a thing.*

Stella was weeping quietly while her grandmother finished. The story *had* hurt. It had wounded them both just in the telling. She leaned over and gave her grandma another gentle hug.

Luby, Maria said. *I am tired, I should have a rest.*

As they walked slowly down the hallway to the bedroom, Stella had one more question. *Grandma, can I ask you about being Jewish? Why did you pretend to be Roman Catholics for so long?*

Pretend? Maria sounded a little indignant. *We didn't pretend.*

I don't understand.

Stella, first we were Jews. Stanislaw and me, we were born Jews. But after the First War, our people were scared. They knew a pogrom could come. So they stopped cutting the boys. They hid their Jewish ways. This was across Poland. They cautioned us in the temples. When the Second War came, we were a little bit protected. And we became Roman Catholics. It was not pretending. Was Jesus the Messiah, who knows? Maybe yes and maybe no. It's not so different to us. But when you are born a Jew, you must die a Jew and that is why.

So many people showed up for Shiva. How did they know?

God is good, luby, and we have many friends here. We are not alone. Others understand. In Canada, many became Jews again, but we did not think it would make such a difference. God is God.

Maria smiled at Stella and sat down heavily on her bed. *Enough. I must sleep a little.*

ADAPTING

D^{ad?}

Hi, Stella. What's up?

I'm at Grandma's.

Is she okay?

Yeah, she's fine. She launched into what Maria had told her about being born Jewish, the words tumbling out.

William was quiet for a moment. *It makes sense.*

She said lots of people knew. Their friends knew. Some of them did the same thing.

Well, I guess it fits. Explains things.

Don't you think it's strange? A little dishonest?

No. I don't. I think it's great, actually. Don't you see? They understood the bigger picture, and they were able to adapt and survive. That takes courage and intelligence.

Really?

I think so. I'm not sure I would have adapted as well as they did. They've been very brave.

You don't think they're phonies?

No! I admire them. Both of them.

I was a little shocked.

Stella, the older you get, the more you'll be shocked by people. People shock the hell out of me sometimes. Good and bad.

But what's going to happen to Grandma? She can't stay here on her own. She'll be lonely. And she'll need help doing things.

I've been thinking about that too. I've talked to Fatima about it.

How is she, Dad?

She's weak, not very strong at all. The treatments exhaust her. And afterwards she's so sick . . .

I'm sorry, I should have asked sooner.

It's okay. Don't worry. But listen, I should probably go. I need to check on Tanner.

Can I do anything?

I don't know, Stella. I can't think. I should go.

Can I come and help with something?

Thanks, Stella. You're already busy enough.

I could fit it in, Dad. Tonight even. Give me the address. It's no trouble.

STELLA AND FATIMA

The house was an impressive three-storey in shades of soft granite. Along its front were four oversized cement planters overflowing with tall red grassy bits, vines, and greenery with vivid, trailing flowers. They looked carefully orchestrated and inviting. Tanner's tricycle was parked in a corner by the three-car garage.

William opened the door when she rang the bell. *Here, Dad, Grandma sent some soup.* Stella passed him a stockpot of rich broth filled with vegetables and chunks of stewing beef.

Bless her. He smiled. *Always trying to feed people.*

Stella took in the surroundings. The front hall was painted in a deep gold that was energetic and bright and felt almost sunny. A sisal mat lay on the foyer's tiled floor and a long Persian carpet ran down the hall. William watched her studying it.

It's one of Fatima's, from Turkey. Nineteenth century. The rug had an almost modern look. There was no fringe, and its abstracted diamonds were delineated by hooked or clawed borders in yellow-gold. The colours of the diamonds themselves alternated between deep burgundy, black, yellow, and red.

It looks modern.

Yes, agreed her father.

Give me something useful to do.

Let's put this away first. William led Stella down the hall to a brightly lit kitchen. The entire back wall was glass and opened up into a small garden. All the colour came from outside—the cupboards and walls were gleaming white, with stainless steel appliances reflecting the light. William opened the fridge and rearranged things to fit the stockpot inside.

Stella looked around. The kitchen flowed into a dining room and then an expansive living room with a cathedral ceiling. It was all in whites and creams except for the carpets, which created sharp contrasts of colour and energy. Tanner was in the living room, absorbed in *Mary Poppins*.

Come on up and see Fatima.

She followed him up the stairs. Another carpet hung in the stairwell landing, and Stella admired the vibrant deep green accent wall it was placed against. *We picked the paint to match the threads. We painted only one wall this colour; it would be too overwhelming otherwise.* The rest of the stairwell was in a sedate cream.

William walked into the bedroom but Stella hung back a bit, not wanting to be intrusive. Fatima looked diminutive in the large bed. It was clear that her hair was thinning and that she'd lost weight since the funeral. *It's so good of you to come,* she said.

I'm sorry you're not well. I just thought I'd see if I could help.

You are welcome here. Fatima smiled. *Please know that this is also your home.*

Stella felt a lump form in her throat and her eyes filled unexpectedly with tears. *Thank you* was all she could say.

Your father tells me that you're also a student of the carpets. He says that you learned a great deal about them with him.

I don't know much, really. But they are beautiful. I love the Turkish one in your hall. With the hook. It's very modern looking.

Yes. The hook denotes waves of water. It's a wish that the traveller would find water. A source of life. I like it too.

And the green prayer rug in the hall, is it a Kerman? I wondered because of the curvilinear floral design. It's very delicate.

Fatima raised an amused eyebrow. *You do know something about rugs. It's a Kerman prayer rug, from the 1840s. That one is very fine. Four hundred knots per inch. The dyes are insect based. It was produced before they started using synthetic dyes for commercial purposes.*

Dad told me you were writing a book on carpets.

Yes, I'd be happy to show it to you when I'm better. Your father tells me that you're a good editor. You might like to look at it?

That would be amazing. I'd love to see it.

Fatima reached out her hand. Stella held it and they smiled at each other. It seemed time to go. She excused herself and went back downstairs, where William soon joined her.

Well, he said, *now that you're here, maybe you can help fold the laundry? I'm no good at folding.*

Absolutely. And I'm looking forward to reading Fatima's book someday.

You might find it interesting. She knows a great deal about carpets. More than I could ever learn.

She was impressed that I guessed the green prayer rug was a Kerman. Stella heard the pride in her voice and felt a little embarrassed.

You've paid close attention for a long time.

They're just so beautiful.

When William opened the door to the laundry room, concealed off one side of the kitchen, Stella saw several baskets filled to overbrimming with clean sheets and towels and children's clothes. They both started in.

You're right, said Stella after a couple of minutes. Her father was fumbling with a big sheet. *You suck at this. Let me do it.*

Okay. Why don't I check on Tanner and warm up some of Maria's soup for dinner?

Deal.

By the time Stella emerged into the kitchen the table had been set for three and hot bowls of soup were already laid out, a cheese sandwich beside one of them. William was straining some soup through a coffee filter into a mug.

I thought the broth might be good for Fatima, but I don't think she'll be able to manage the meat right now. Why don't you and Tanner start and I'll join you in a few minutes.

Stella stepped into the living room and waited for Tanner to notice her. Then she picked up the remote control. *Tanner, if you help me push this button, we can stop the movie until after supper.* He stood up and looked at the button, carefully extended his forefinger, and pushed it.

What a big boy, Stella enthused in her teacher voice. *You are so smart.* Tanner smiled and then followed her into the kitchen, climbing up on one of the chairs. They ate together a little awkwardly. Stella kept looking at her trusting little brother, marvelling still that she'd suddenly found this tiny person in her life.

Tanner ate the cheese sandwich by himself, but then looked at Stella expectantly.

Do you want help with your soup?

He nodded.

She picked up Tanner's spoon. *Blow,* he instructed. On they went from there until he'd downed the bowl. She'd been a little clumsy, and between them they did manage to spill some soup on his shirt and face. Still, Stella felt proud.

Tanner slipped off the chair. *Mary Poppins?* He reached for Stella's hand.

PERSPECTIVE

When Stella got home that night she told Pam about taking Maria grocery shopping. She kept her grandmother's stories to herself.

She's managing?

Yes, but she seems pretty lonely. I'm not sure everything has sunk in.

She'll have to get used to it. Lots of us live alone.

She misses Grandpa.

Stella, I'm warning you, if you start doing everything for her she'll begin to depend on you and then you'll be stuck. Trapped into doing things. That's why I haven't gone yet. We'll have a visit next week. But I'm not going to go every day. I can't change my life around.

No, Mom, no one would expect you to. Least of all Grandma.

You say that now, but trust me, when she wants to be manipulative, she'll get her way. She isn't as nice as you think she is, you know. You and your father, you've both always thought they're perfect. They're not! And I ought to know. They get exactly what they want and it doesn't matter what they do to get it.

That's an awful thing to say!

It's true. How do you think they survived the war? Do you honestly believe that innocent people survived without hurting anyone? Not a chance. Your grandfather killed people and your grandmother had to spread her legs. They're not who you think they are.

I can't believe you're saying this.

I'm telling you for your own good. Don't get sucked in.

Mom, you're just being mean. Grandma loves me.

Of course she loves you. She just has a screwball perspective sometimes, Stella. Like when I was pregnant with you, for instance. Your father was over the moon with excitement, but I was scared. I'd never had a baby before and no one told me what to expect. So I told Maria how afraid I was and you know what she said?

Stella shook her head.

She said, "Look Pamela, don't be so selfish. The whole German army came and so will this one."

Stella smiled.

It's not funny, Stella. She's just totally into her own story all the time. You have to find things to do with people your own age.

STELLA AND TARA

Back in her room, Stella found herself shaking with the hate-fulness of what her mother had said. *How ironic*, she raged, *that Pam would lecture me about not getting sucked into other people's expectations*. She needed to get out, to get in the car and just drive. She couldn't stay here with this anger burning inside her. And yet what was most troubling, if she was honest with herself, was the question her mother had raised. Her grandparents were survivors, they'd even hidden their Jewishness to survive, so what else had they been forced to do? Stella wasn't sure she wanted to know. The pain of such suffering and the price of their survival were perhaps best kept in their past. How could anyone really understand what had taken place during that dark time?

She drove randomly at first—around town, past the main street, north along Cemetery Road. She found herself going by the new subdivision, where most of the houses were still framed with plywood. You could see, though, that they were spacious and set among gently rolling hills. Now she was heading towards the old Quaker Meeting House, near Tara's. It was late, but she pulled over anyway and gave her call. *Feel like a drive?*

Sure. Where to?

I'll pick you up in a minute.

Stella made a big loop around the Meeting House, circled back to Tara's, and pulled into the driveway to wait.

Hey, what's up?

My mother.

What did she do this time?

Stella poured it all out as she drove aimlessly along back roads. She knew she could count on Tara to understand, to ask the thoughtful questions she was known for. Tara had always been the charismatic one, the irreverent one, but she had a fun-damental level-headedness that grounded her. They talked for a long time. Stella could feel the weight begin to lift.

Then Tara seemed to hesitate. It was clear she had something on her mind.

You know what I think?

What?

I think the time is right for us to buy a townhouse together. You know, one of those I told you about in that new subdivision. I've looked around at other places, Stella. Those townhouses are a good price. They're not far from town. And they're really nice.

But who would look after Pam?

Oh, Stella, we've discussed this. Maybe her zillion doctors could look after her, along with anyone else we can talk into it. Honestly, this is a step you need take.

I feel guilty just thinking about it.

Screw that. You're never going to please her anyway. C'mon, you know that's the truth.

I do.

So say it. Say: "Okay, Tara you're right. I'm in. Let's get a place." Tara grinned at her hopefully.

Stella thought about what Tara was offering. A chance to make a break. She had a steady teaching job; getting a mortgage shouldn't be difficult. She had no debts, and had some money saved, including the holiday funds her grandparents had given her. If she needed it, her father would likely co-sign. With her and Tara's incomes combined, they could do this. It would be amazing to have a place of their own, she thought. A place she could paint and decorate and fill with the things she loved. A place that she and Tara could call *theirs*. A place to invite friends over. Stella couldn't remember the last time she'd felt free to do that. Tara was right. And, in her own way, even Pam had been encouraging her to get on with her life.

She pulled over onto the side of the road for a second time and looked at Tara. *You're right. I'm in. Let's do it!* Tara leaned over and hugged her.

I knew you'd come 'round. Awesome!

They decided that on Monday after work they'd visit the sales office for the new subdivision. In the meantime, Tara would call a friend at the bank and talk to her about mortgage rates.

Late that night Stella lay in bed, her head still spinning. She began inventorying the furniture they would need. She thought about accent walls like the ones at her father's house; maybe she could clean and hang her star carpet. She fell asleep thinking of colour schemes and furniture and the fun they'd have decorating and entertaining. She might even invite some people from work over for a drink one night.

THE TOWNHOUSE

Stella drove directly from work to the sales office and waited for Tara. The lot was unpaved and muddy. The office was a construction trailer of sorts, with fancy skirting and expensive signs nailed all over it. Bright pink and green flags fluttered on a nearby flagpole. This amused Stella: what country had pink and green flags? These particular ones represented a new adventure and a new beginning. A country that was hers to conquer.

When Tara arrived they went inside and sat down in two tiny office chairs. *I'll be right with you* came a male voice from behind a partition. The voice was followed by a handsome young man with dark, wavy hair and navy suit. Stella had the vague feeling that she'd seen him before. Tara glanced sideways at her. Maybe she thought so too.

He walked them out to a model home that stood at the end of a short row of townhouses. It had been completely furnished and had three bedrooms, one bathroom, a powder room on the main floor, an unfinished basement, and a huge combined kitchen and dining room. The living room was a walk-out to a postage stamp of a backyard. It was perfect.

We can use the third bedroom as an office and put in two desks, said Tara.

We can get a barbecue and picnic table for the backyard.

We'll need some furniture.

It doesn't have to be new.

The salesman, Frank, stepped to the side to let them talk. Stella noticed him out of the corner of her eye. He was obviously ADHD; he kept touching things and moving around impulsively. She'd taught enough students to recognize the signs. It was a little distracting. He was a really good-looking man, though.

When they walked back to the trailer, Frank introduced them to an associate. *He'll draw up the paperwork,* he said. *I was just helping out. I didn't want two beautiful women to have to wait around.*

Tara sighed a little too audibly, evidently smitten with his charm. Frank left them in the trailer with Mr. Grainger, who pulled out sheaves of paper and started filling them in.

Stella cleared her throat. *Who was that?*

Frank Dinapoli. He's the project manager. He doesn't usually deal with the customers, but he likes to help out. He's a great guy.

Tara looked at Stella with a quizzical expression. They both recognized the name.

BREAKING NEWS I

As soon as Stella got back in her car, she phoned her father and told him all about it.

That's fantastic. I'm proud of you. Have you told your mother?

Not yet. But I will tonight. And you know, I think she might just approve.

Well, that's good to hear.

Dad, I'm so happy. I can't believe it. The deal closes in thirty days.

It's great news. I'm so pleased. But buying your first house can be expensive. Let me know if you need anything.

I've got a good job, Dad. You don't need to worry about me.

It's a parent's right to worry, Stella.

BREAKING NEWS II

Stella was still glowing when she walked in the front door. *Mom, guess what?* Without waiting for Pam to respond, she spilled it out.

Pam looked at her strangely. *Just like that? You didn't think you should tell me about it first?*

I'm telling you now. And I'm so excited. She grabbed her mother by both hands and spun her around the kitchen.

Pam staggered a bit after the spin and then righted herself. She smiled at Stella. *Well then if you got what you wanted, that's good. I hope you didn't pay too much for it. But you and Tara know everything about these things, I suppose.*

What's the matter, Mom? Aren't you happy for me?

Of course I'm happy for you. I just think you could have talked to me about it first. I'm not stupid, you know. I may have had some advice or something useful to contribute.

I just thought it was time to make a decision to become more independent. I thought you'd be proud of me.

I'm glad you're finally doing something you want to do. That's really good news.

Honest, Mom, you're not mad?

Why should I be mad? I've been telling you to be more independent. You can't always mope around with me and your grandmother. You're young. You don't want to miss out on things.

I'm so happy.

Good. After dinner, maybe you can check the basement to see if you want any of the old furniture down there. Take whatever. It'll be something to start with.

BREAKING NEWS III

Fatima was still bedridden. The cancer treatments had ravaged her features and taken her lovely hair and all her energy. She slept a lot. William had moved a television into the bedroom, but she never wanted to watch it. Tanner sometimes crawled up on the bed to snuggle with her, but even this seemed to drain her of what little strength she had.

William went upstairs after Stella's telephone call. *You'll never believe what Stella just told me.* He was grinning. *She and her friend Tara have bought a townhouse together.*

Fatima smiled at him and reached out her hand. William clasped it and drew near to her side. She spoke softly; he had to bend down to hear her words. *I want you to give her the green Kerman for her new house. She liked it when she was here.*

William was surprised. *Are you sure? It's pretty valuable. We even painted the wall for it.*

We can repaint the wall. I want her to have it. From me. Promise me you'll do this?

Yes, of course. He studied her face intently. *Are you feeling okay? Are you in pain? Can I get you something?*

No. I'm fine. Just tired. I need to rest. But promise me, William?

I promise.

SWIMMING

Pam heard Stella showering and getting ready for school. She didn't feel like getting up yet. Anyway, Stella liked her own space in the mornings; she was always grumpy for about the first hour. Better to wait till she was off. It was good that Stella was moving out. To be on her own before she lost what few looks she had. Just last week, when Pam had suggested that some yoga wouldn't hurt her figure, Stella went nuts. Apparently she was being too critical. How on earth were you supposed to help someone if they took everything you said the wrong way?

She waited until she heard the door shut before starting her day. Her physiotherapist had given her fifteen minutes of stretches to do. They were supposed to help keep her limber, and they seemed to be helping. He'd also proposed swimming as a good way to maintain some muscle tone. And so last week she'd gone to the pool for the first time in years. She'd bought a new suit first, a sharp royal blue one-piece. It was cut nicely, and she liked how it showed off her figure.

Pam walked leisurely through the parking lot to the sports complex. The building was filled with young people and she scanned their firm bodies critically, comparing herself only slightly unfavourably to only some of the girls. Her goal was to swim four laps, rest, and then shoot for four more. It wasn't much, but it was a start. She loved the feel of the water on her legs and arms. She concentrated on her strokes, her technique, her breathing. The rhythm was relaxing. Pam felt good.

After her fourth lap, she rested in the shallow end and gazed around at some of the swimmers churning away. The chlorine was pungent, but she didn't mind that either. It made her remember to rinse her suit out thoroughly so the bright colour wouldn't fade. The diving board thwanged and she looked down the length of the pool. A man in a tiny black Speedo had just done a very high dive and people had stopped to watch. He appeared to have good form. Pam didn't know a lot about such things.

The man climbed out of the pool and sprang back up the steps to the high board. He bounced several times at its edge and then jumped, curling his upper body backwards towards his butt and spreading his arms like wings. It was incredibly graceful to watch. A few onlookers applauded. Pam stared at him. It couldn't be. There was something about the way he'd sprung up those steps that caught at her heart.

PAM AND TONY

Pam stayed in the shallow end and watched Tony dive again and again. He was a natural showman. He'd bow to the onlookers when they clapped and sometimes even salute from the board before he jumped. He seemed inexhaustible. She knew she had to get out of the water; her fingers were starting to prune. The question was, *What to do?* He hadn't called her since he'd left the house angry more than a month ago. Not that she was surprised. He was the sort of guy who just cut and run when things got difficult. That was his nature.

Calculating carefully, she waited until his next dive then sped up the metal stairs and directly into the changing room. There was no way she'd let him see her. He had such an ego he'd probably think she was following him.

She showered and changed but didn't take the time to put on her makeup or dry her hair. Too risky. Hurrying, she grabbed her things and walked quickly back to her car. Then she heard her name. *Pam. Hey, Pam!* She got in, locked the door, turned on the ignition, and began to reverse out of the spot. There was a pounding on her trunk lid. She hesitated. *Hey, Pam, it's me. Didn't you see me? I thought I recognized your car.* Tony was behind her, waving his arms like a windmill. He was hard to ignore. She pulled back in, turned off the ignition, and rolled down the window.

Tony sprinted up and ducked his head in. *Hey Pam. How are you? You been swimming? I come here every morning. First I jog the track—it's one of those rubber things, you know, low impact on your joints—and then I swim for an hour.* He gave her one of his big grins, clearly pleased with himself.

That's nice, Tony. I'm sure it's good for you.

Yeah. For sure. Did you see me diving?

No. I didn't notice. I was trying to swim my laps.

Well, I'm pretty good. Me and Frankie joined a club up north when he was a kid. He was like a goddamn seal. Had to do something with him.

I should go.

What's your hurry? Wanna go for a coffee or breakfast or something?

Pam looked at him. He was wearing track pants, obviously just pulled on over his Speedo. He hadn't bothered to dry himself properly. He was standing there looking like an overgrown kid. His T-shirt was damp and clung to his chest and she could see a pot belly starting to bulge ever so slightly. She hadn't noticed this before. The neck of the T-shirt was stretched out of shape, and she could also see fine grey chest hairs curling up around the base of his throat.

I don't think so, Tony.

What? You still mad at me?

Pam got out of the car and stood with her hands on her hips. She was uncomfortable having him talking down to her. She felt disadvantaged. *What do you want from me, Tony?*

He sighed. *I want you to tell me the truth, Pam. I hate being lied to.*

You don't have the right to ask me those kinds of questions. You're an overgrown child who takes no responsibility for your actions. You just

*do whatever the hell you want and expect everyone to be delighted with
you. I goddamn hate you and never want to see you again.*

*Is that so? Well, I hate goddamn liars. There's one thing I can't
stand and it's a goddamn liar.*

*Good. Then leave me the hell alone and let me out of this goddamn
parking space.* Pam reached for the door handle and was about to
get back in her car. Tony blocked her with his arm. *Move your
goddamn arm.*

Tony started to laugh. *I can't.* He put both arms on her door
and leaned his weight on them. He was really laughing now. *You
sure got a way of talking to a guy*, he sputtered.

Despite herself, Pam smiled.

*C'mon, Pam. Let's not be mad. Let's go have breakfast or some-
thing and talk.*

I can't. My hair is a mess.

*Then let me make it. We can go to Frankie's. I'll fry us some eggs.
Can you cook?*

*Yeah. I had to learn. C'mon, follow my truck and we'll just have
breakfast. Then you can swear at me some more and we can talk this
through.* He grinned at her. It was impossible not to give in.

FRANKIE'S PLACE

Pam followed the truck back to Waldham and into the edge
of the new subdivision north of town. She was fuming mad,
but also curious and a little bit excited.

She parked behind the truck and got out. The driveway and
property were still muddy. The sod hadn't been laid yet, or the
driveway paved. Still, a very nicely finished house had risen out
of the muck. It even appeared to have window treatments already
in place. A large silver trailer was parked next to it.

Tony stood at the front door waiting. He held it open for
her and smacked her bottom when she walked through. *I'm
glad you came*, he said. *I gotta get out of my wet suit or my balls are
gonna shrivel. I'll be right back.* He bounded off down the hallway.

Pam looked around. The place was immaculate: no dust, everything tidy and in its place. The decorating was not to her taste, with oversized leather furniture and slabs of thick pine everywhere, but it was nicely done. She went to the fridge and pulled out eggs, a tomato, green pepper, milk, butter, cheese. *Do you want an omelette?* she called to Tony.

Great. I'll be right there.

Pam heard the shower starting. She found a bowl and began her preparations. She was just tipping the mixture into a hot frying pan when Tony reappeared. He was once more nicely dressed in khaki pants and a striped dress shirt. He hadn't put on socks and she noticed his bare feet. Suddenly it seemed intimate to be standing in a man's kitchen making an omelette while he was beside her in bare feet. She felt her face flushing.

Tony looked at her quizzically. *You still mad?*

Yes, she said. *I'm still mad.*

Okay then. Let's eat first and talk later.

Is it always so easy for you, Tony Dinapoli? Do you always manage to charm your way through every situation?

Yeah, pretty much. He sat down in a kitchen chair, reached for Pam, and pulled her down into his lap. He kissed her ear. She struggled to get up. He whispered, *I'm hoping you don't stay mad for too long.*

Pam stood. *The omelette . . .*

As she busied herself at the stove Tony stood up too. *It smells good.*

They divided the omelette onto two plates and carried them through to the living room. Tony sat on the couch and put his feet up on the coffee table while he ate.

Did Rita let you do that?

Do what?

Put your feet on the coffee table.

He nodded. *I'm guessing your husband was more refined?*

Yes, he was. He would never do that.

Well, at least I don't have a pickle in my ass.

William didn't have a pickle in his ass.

I didn't mean William.

What? How dare you?

I call it the way I see it. You are a woman who is in some serious need of something.

Oh, and you're the expert all of a sudden? And what exactly do you think I need?

I haven't figured that out yet. But when I do, I'll let you know.

Pam glared at him and stomped her foot in frustration.

Tony looked at her. *Did you just stomp your foot at me?*

So what if I did?

Oh my God. Do it again. Tony laughed. *Do you always do that when you're mad?*

She glowered. *You are a very frustrating man!*

And you are a very frustrating woman with a pickle in her ass!

Tony got up from the couch and crossed over to her chair. He reached out both hands and pulled her up so that she was standing in front of him. *The problem here,* he said, *is that we have to get the sex out of the way. Then we can talk.*

You are the last person in the world I want to have sex with. Pam pushed him away.

He stepped closer. She could feel his breath. *You want to have sex with me too. You want to know if we're going to be any good together. You want to know what it's like to get naked with me after all these years.*

What I'm wondering is what makes you think you're so irresistible.

Tony stepped a fraction of an inch closer but still did not touch her. He leaned over and whispered, *You are a beautiful woman and I want to be with you. I want to taste you all over. I want to touch you and hold you. But not if you don't want me to.* It wasn't his joking, flirty voice. He sounded huskier, more serious.

Pam was quivering. The energy between them was almost unbearable. She moved towards him and he took her hands in his and led her slowly down the hall.

THE HOSPITAL

Stella was still asleep in bed when her cell phone rang at six in the morning. It was her father. *Stella, I had to take Fatima to the hospital. Tanner is with me. Could you come by and pick him up? I'm at the Trillium Health Centre.*

She swung into action. She called the school and left a message saying she wouldn't be in and that her lesson plans were on her desk. Then she pulled on some clothes, rushed downstairs, and left Pam a note. *Had to go out. See you tonight.*

Stella drove quickly. She had a vague notion of where the hospital was, and after exiting on the Queensway, simply followed the blue signs. She parked and then ran in the direction of the red *Emergency* sign. An attractive-looking couple were standing near her father in the waiting room. Tanner was sleeping peacefully on a couch, covered in William's trench coat and clutching his Wojtek bear.

Dad?

William turned. Relief eased his worried face. *Oh, Stella, thank you for coming.* He opened his arms and hugged her. *This is Parisa and Parvez. They're Fatima's cousins and co-workers. Parisa has been a sister to her.* Stella shook hands with them, noticing how well dressed they were but also how agitated.

What happened?

She was sick. Kept throwing up. Then I noticed she was throwing up small amounts of blood so I brought her here to have things checked out. She's pretty weak.

I'm glad you called. I'll take Tanner home, if that's what you were thinking. Is there anything special I should know? Allergies or anything?

No. Just be careful with cookies and treats. We try to make sure he doesn't eat too much junk. He's pretty easy. He likes TV and music and dancing. Maybe you could take him to Indian Grove.

That's a great idea, Dad. I'll head to Grandma's. Do I need the car seat?

Yes. You do. Take my car and leave me yours. That's easier than switching it. I'll walk you out.

When they got to the car, William woke Tanner up slowly. *That's a good boy. Your big sister is here. She's going to take you to Grandma's. Won't that be fun? Okay, c'mon big boy, you be good for your sister.* Tanner opened his eyes and smiled but then fell fast asleep again as soon as William buckled him into the car seat.

After kissing her goodbye her father scurried back to the emergency entrance, his shoulders tense. Stella took a minute to check the knobs and adjust the mirrors and then drove carefully out onto the highway. She tended to be a fast driver, and prided herself on having good reflexes and defensive driving skills. Today, though, she was nervous. She'd never driven with a child in the car. A precious, sleeping child. Her brother.

As she approached High Park she pulled into an empty lot and called her grandmother. *Sure, sure, come,* Maria kept repeating, and was already waving from the wide open door by the time Stella drove up. When William had strapped Tanner in she'd watched closely so that she'd know how to get him out; now, she pushed the release button and carefully lifted the restraints over his head. Then she stroked his cheek with her finger. *Tanner, we're at Grandma's. Will you wake up for Grandma?*

Tanner roused slowly and gave Stella a sleepy smile. She reached in to lift him and he clung to her easily, his arms wrapped around her neck as if it were the most natural thing in the world. She bent her head and inhaled—baby powder, baby shampoo, and something else she couldn't identify, something more exotic— before transferring him to Maria. The weight of him, the smell of him, his trust, did something to Stella. The sensation surprised her. For the second time in two days she felt tears stinging her eyes.

WAITING

Maria must have known something was wrong. She glanced at Stella over Tanner's head with concern. *Inside, come, we have a coffee.* She carried Tanner down the hall and laid him down on her bed. He rolled over to one side and curled up, falling quickly asleep again. Stella stood in the hallway watching him, admiring how easily he adapted. Then she followed Maria to the kitchen.

Tell me, what is happened?

Stella sat down at the Formica table and toyed with the geraniums in the bud vase. *Fatima is sick. Dad had to take her to the hospital. I think it's serious. She was throwing up blood.*

Maria considered for a moment. *So it has gotten worse. Your father has told me how unwell she has been. Well, then she is in the right place. The doctors will know what to do. She is a young woman. They will help her.*

I hope so, Gran. Dad looked pretty freaked out.

Come, we have some coffee, and in a little while the boy will wake up and we will have a nice day. Maria began to busy herself with the percolator. *You know, Stan and me danced at their wedding. At first, I did not want to go. I thought it wasn't good to do it. Pamela, I thought, she would be upset. But Stan, Stan said we should celebrate with William. So I went. I had a new dress, I can show you. Fatima was a beautiful bride. She kissed us both and said we were her new family. Your father was so happy, luby. You should have seen how happy.*

I wish I'd gone.

Ach, your mother, she wouldn't let you. Such stupidness. She is become a small person. Selfish. I don't know what happened to her.

You know what happened. Dad left her.

Your father left, Stella, because there was no reason to stay.

What are you saying?

Maria sat down heavily at the table, reached across it, and took Stella's hand. *Your father, luby, is a good man. An honourable man. He deserves much happiness. Your mother tricked him into marrying. Stanislaw figured it out. We did not want to believe it but it was true.*

Stella felt goosebumps rising on her arms. The hair on the back of her neck felt strange and a sick feeling in her stomach began. *What do you mean? What are you saying?*

Your mother was not pure when she married. She had been with other boys before your father. She was already carrying you. And William married her.

What? Are you telling me that Dad isn't my father?

Of course he is your father. Who else raised you and feeds you and loves you? William is your father. But maybe, who knows, maybe William didn't make you.

Stella's heart was pounding now. *Grandma, how can you say this to me? Now you tell me this?*

I telling you these things, luby, so you know how good is William. What a fine man. He loves you. But it is time you should know about Pamela. She will do what is good for Pamela. She does not care if she tricks a good man.

Stella struggled to absorb what her grandmother was telling her. She didn't *look* like William particularly, her colouring was much darker, but then Pam's colouring was dark too. She was a lot *like* her father though, their temperaments, their way of thinking. He had always understood her.

She looked intently at her grandmother. *Does Dad know?*

No, luby, and we will not tell him. He has other things more important to think about. This is history.

Then why tell me now?

Because it is your history, luby.

I don't understand.

Your mother is my daughter and I love her, but I know who she is. You are young. You must make your own life. Your grandfather and me, we have talked of this many times.

I've already decided to move out, Gran. My friend Tara and I are going to buy a townhouse together. We've saved enough money.

Good. That is good. You are young and smart and have an education. You can do things with your life. Instead of watching the TV and dreaming about movie stars. You can do everything.

Stella nodded. *I know.*

Stanislaw will be happy. He knows, luby. He still knows. I talk to him still. He is watching.

I think I hear Tanner, said Stella. They both got up and walked softly down the hallway. Tanner was sitting up on the bed, rubbing his eyes. He smiled to see them and slid down to the floor. Maria grabbed him up in a big hug.

Would you like some breakfast? she asked. The little boy nodded and all three trooped back to the kitchen where Maria began to bustle about. Cereal, toast, milk, sliced apple. Tanner sat at his place at the table, pumping his legs back and forth as though on a swing. He seemed a little confused by the change in his routine but didn't ask any questions. Stella felt compelled to keep looking at him, feeling strangely protective, wanting to make sure he wasn't upset.

A TIME OF MOURNING

William left the hospital late in the afternoon. Parisa and Parvez walked out to the parking lot with him. He couldn't find his car. He walked up and down looking for it until he remembered. *Stella,* he thought. *Tanner. My God. What do I tell Tanner?*

William began to cry. Deep racking sobs from his core. He bent over, his stomach muscles strained, his lungs gasping for air. He put his hands on his knees and folded himself downward.

This was surely a dream. Nobody just hemorrhages and dies in a hospital. Surely to God there was a mistake. He tried to gulp down his grief, to take in some air. He straightened himself and looked at Parisa and Parvez. They too were crying. Now they all three lunged towards each other, clinging to one another, shaking. *Twenty-four hours ago things were normal, happy. They were fine. Fatima was recovering. How could it have changed so drastically? How could her life be taken so quickly?*

We will tell the family, said Parvez. *You should go home, try to rest.*

William looked at him stupidly. *I don't know what to do. Where should I go?*

Go home, said Parisa. *We'll check in on you later.*

But Tanner . . .

He'll be fine, said Parvez. *Your daughter has him. He'll be fine for now. You need some rest.* Parvez took Stella's key fob from William's hand. He clicked the alarm button and listened for its sound. Then he guided William to Stella's car. *Can you drive?*

Yes, I can drive.

Good, said Parisa. *Go straight home. We'll be by later.*

William kissed them both and got into the car. He pushed the seat back and stretched his legs. He adjusted the mirrors. He sat. *Don't think,* he said to himself. *Don't think and don't feel. First you must drive. Drive home. Then you will drink some scotch and lie down on the couch. Then you will decide what to do next. Don't think. Just drive.*

He unlocked the door and went into the house. It seemed quiet. He'd left all the lights on in his hurry, and now he walked from room to room turning them off, inventorying the empty spaces. He approached their bedroom last. The lovely paprika walls shouted at him: "She's not here." He stopped in the doorway, afraid to enter. Slowly he walked forward, his steps hesitant and halting. He stood by her side of the bed. The shape of her was still there, in the sheets and on the pillow. He looked at it carefully, measuring the length and width of her with his eyes. He bent down and smelled the pillow. A hint of jasmine. *How was this possible?*

He began to weep. And then, surrendering to his exhaustion, he dropped to the floor and curled into himself.

Hours later he woke, stiff and confused. It was dark outside. As he started to get up he noticed a sheaf of printed pages on the floor under the bed. He gathered them and stood. It was part of her manuscript. William held the pages in disbelief. These were her words. This was her project. But she was gone. Only the paper remained. And Tanner. That was all he had left of her. He shook his head slowly with the incredulity of it all. Part of her legacy was in his hands and he had no way to deal with it. To deal with her loss. He had no way forward. No way to fix this. He clenched and unclenched his free hand.

William carried the pages to her office and laid them reverently on her desk. He sat in her chair and looked around the room. Family photos were pinned to a bulletin board . . . pictures taken in happier times. Pictures of them together on the beach, pictures of their newborn son. William reached up and touched the glossy images in disbelief. This was it. This was all there was left. Through the sheer lace curtain, the headlights of a car passed by on the road. William was struck by this. *How could someone be driving a car casually by their house? How was it possible that the world had continued to turn?*

He looked back at the desk and picked up the manuscript. He traced his fingers over the text and then flipped the pages slowly, looking for traces of her, evidence of her touch.

Before the weaving of a carpet would begin, the pattern was chosen. The wool and the cotton threads were bought separately and then taken to the master dyer. The loom would be carefully prepared and the underlying structure of the carpet set with the strong threads. An entire family would have input into the size and coloration of the carpet. Each of these decisions represented an important economic factor: How many people and how many months of labour would be required to complete the work before it could be trimmed and pressed and sold? How many dyes must be mixed and paid for before the dyer would colour the wool? In short, what would be the return on investment for this carpet, and how ambitious a project could the family unit afford to undertake?

In addition to these important financial considerations, a much more significant question would be addressed: What message do we wish to communicate in the carpet we weave? What statement will we convey in the iconography and symbols we select? Will this carpet speak to the beauty of creation or to the strife of war? Will this carpet bring a blessing to a household?

The families who wove these carpets were cohesive units: each member of the family would have a prescribed role in the decision making and in the craft of it. Additionally, certain families would demonstrate an affinity for specific motifs: niches, medallions, palmettes, flowers, octagons, guls, stripes, stars, compartments, borders, and lattices. Again, all members of the family would have expertise with certain components and would be called upon, at the appropriate interval, to contribute their skill.

Families are often complex and dynamic groupings, required to constantly embrace new members but also to mourn the loss of those who have departed. The timeless legacy of their work can be valued and cherished as representative of the joy and the heartache that converge when disparate . . .

William read her words slowly. He read them a second time. *Did she know that a time of mourning was about to descend?* He sat on the bed and considered. *Why had she begun to write about the family in this way? Was she trying to tell him something?* A desperate idea began to form in his mind. A way of keeping her close.

The sound of the doorbell interrupted William's thoughts. Still carrying the pages, he went downstairs and opened the door to Parisa and Parvez. *Come in. How are her parents?*

Parisa looked down with an almost imperceptible shake of her head.

They were all silent for a moment. Then Parvez looked at William. *How are you?*

Look at this, he said instead of answering. He passed Parisa the manuscript pages. *I just found it.*

Parisa stared at him, trying to focus on what he was saying. But she took the pages, then followed William to the kitchen with them. *Have you called your daughter?*

Oh God. No. I fell asleep.

Do you want me to call? asked Parvez.

No, I should, just give me a minute. I need a drink first. William took down the bottle of scotch and poured himself a finger of the golden liquid. He gestured at Parvez. *Help yourself. I'll call her now.*

SAD NEWS

Stella was fighting down panic by the time her father called. It was ten-thirty at night and Tanner was once more asleep. They'd played in the park, visited the little zoo, eaten an ice cream cone, and watched TV. It had been a very full day, and Tanner had asked for Mummy and Daddy only a couple of times. *Daddy will come soon,* Stella had promised. Maria was grim. William wouldn't be gone this long if all was well. It wasn't like him to be thoughtless.

Dad? Where are you?

I'm at home, Stella. I needed to rest for a bit.

Are you okay, how's Fatima?

I'm okay, how is Tanner? Was he a good boy?

He's been great, Dad. He asked for you, though.

Is he sleeping?

Yes, we put him down on Grandma's bed.

Okay, then . . .

What's wrong?

Maria heard the worry in Stella's voice and came over to stand next to her. She strained to listen.

Stella, this is hard . . . It's Fatima. She's not coming home . . .

Stella was silent, absorbing his words, trying to understand
what he was telling her. She looked at her grandmother. Maria
was shaking her head slowly, her aged hands holding her cheeks.
She began to sway with the shaking.

Dad?

She hemorrhaged . . . They couldn't save her.

Oh, God. Dad, I'm so sorry.

*I know . . . Stella. Listen, can you keep Tanner there tonight? I
have some things I have to do. I'll come in the morning. I should be there
when he wakes up.*

Sure, Dad. Anything. Are you okay?

Yes. Parisa and Parvez are with me.

Stella put her arms around her grandmother. They both
began to cry. *The poor little libhober*, Maria kept repeating, *the poor
little libhober.*

At length Stella extracted herself, wiping her face with the palms
of her hands. She checked on Tanner, she spoke to her mother,
she called the school. Then she joined Maria in the kitchen.
Despite the hour, her grandmother was busy making perogies.

Perogies, Grandma?

Sure. Perogies. We have to eat.

Stella smiled. *Okay, can I help?*

The cheese needs grating, if you want.

Stella found a big block of cheddar in the fridge. Maria had
already set out the grater and a bowl. She hated using the grater;
she always managed to scrape a knuckle or make her hands bleed.
No extra meat, Grandpa Lipinski used to joke. Stella smiled again
remembering.

TONY AND FRANKIE

*Ya know, Frankie, I've known her a long time. We both grew up in
High Park before I moved to Sudbury. I want you to meet her.*

*Dad, this is crazy. What makes you think you can pick up where
you left off twenty-five years ago? People change. This woman can't be
the same girl you used to know. God knows what you're getting into.*

Frankie, listen, this is a new chance for me. A chance to maybe find some companionship. How can it hurt? We're just going to take a holiday. We'll take the trailer to California. We'll see some sights. Spend some time together. A month, maybe six weeks.

Dad, I don't want you to get hurt. I don't like to see you rushing into something.

Frankie, listen to me. I'm forty-five years old and I'm a recovering alcoholic and my prostate don't work so well and I'm alone. You have your whole life ahead of you. I don't got so many chances left.

FINISHING THE BOOK

William hung up the phone and gulped down the last of his scotch. He went back to the kitchen and poured himself another one. Parisa and Parvez were at the kitchen table, also drinking scotch. William sat down. Fatima's pages were there on the table. He picked them up. *Do you think she knew?*

Parvez shook his head. *How could she know?*

She knew, said Parisa. *Why else would she say that? It has nothing to do with carpets.*

William nodded. *She had most of the first draft written, I think.* He was speaking rapidly, intently. *It's on her laptop.* He jumped up.

Parisa and Parez could hear him pounding up the stairs. They looked at each other wonderingly.

William returned quickly, placing Fatima's laptop on the table between them. When he opened it, they could see that his hands were shaking. Then the screen saver appeared: a lovely photograph that Parisa had taken of Fatima, William, and Tanner on his fourth birthday. William sobbed at the sight of it.

Parisa's own tears begin to stream again. But slowly she reached for the keyboard, opened the documents folder, and found a file, last updated days before, called CarpetsofDelight. The three of them leaned in together. It began with what looked like progress notes: *Introduction – done; Chapter 1 – A Cultural*

History – done, Chapter 2 – Regional Specialties – done; Chapter 3 – Symbolism and Iconography – done; Chapter 4 – Care and Maintenance – incomplete; Chapter 5 – Valuation – incomplete; Chapter 6 – Decorator's Gallery – text complete but many pictures missing; Conclusion – not started. What followed were well over a hundred pages of text.

Well, that's that, then, said Parvez, slapping the table with his hand. *It's not ready.*

William turned his gaze to Parisa. She gazed back at him. Neither was willing to surrender it as a hopeless task. Parisa understood now: the book would be a way of completing something Fatima had started, a way of honouring her. William put his hand on the laptop. *I know how to finish this,* he said urgently, *if you'll help me.*

Parisa looked at him quizzically. *Yes?*

My daughter has always loved the carpets, and she's an English teacher. If you help me write the missing pieces, I think Stella might help us edit it. Parvez could do Valuation, I can finish the Care and Maintenance piece, and Parisa can collect the last of the pictures. And when that's done, we can write the Conclusion.

Then I'll get the last of the pictures, said Parisa. *We'll finish Fatima's book together.*

They smiled at each another, and Parisa reached across the table to hold his hand.

Finally they looked at Parvez. He nodded. *Then it's agreed,* he said sombrely. *We will finish the book.*

THE REQUEST

William arrived at the Indian Grove house early the next morning. He was desperate to see his son, to hold him in his arms. When he pulled up he saw that the side door was open, and without knocking he walked in. Maria and Stella were in the kitchen, waiting. Together, they held him tightly. He felt himself choking up again and broke free of them gently. *I'll go see Tanner,* he said, heading down the hallway.

Daddy! they heard. *Hi, Daddy!* They looked at each other thoughtfully.

I will make breakfast, said Maria, *and a nice cup of coffee.*

But they stood there, not moving. They didn't know if they'd hear Tanner cry for his mummy or if they'd be silent witness to the sound of William's grief. They were braced for an onslaught of pain they could not alleviate.

William rejoined them, carrying Tanner, after twenty minutes. Both had been crying, but Tanner seemed to have forgotten why. He reached out to his grandma, who smothered him with kisses. Stella clutched his small hand and bent her forehead to its warmth. *I think*, said William, *that this little man should be allowed to watch cartoons while he waits for his breakfast. What do you think?*

Maria smiled. William carried Tanner through to the living room and turned on the TV. Stella stood frozen, not knowing how to help or what to do.

It is all right, luby, said her grandmother. *We look after the living.* Stella began to set the table for breakfast. She poured her father a big mug of coffee with milk and sugar, just the way he liked it, and brought it in to him.

William took it from her and motioned her to the couch, once more draped in a sheet, and they sat down beside each other. *I have a favour to ask, something that is very important to me.*

Anything.

You know that Fatima was writing a book when she died. It's called Carpets of Delight. *It was very special to her.* He paused and breathed deeply, and then spoke again. *She didn't have a chance to finish it.*

Stella looked at him, wondering.

I want to finish it for her, but I'm no writer. Parisa will help me, and Parvez.

She waited quietly.

I wondered if you would help with the editing.

Stella reached for his hand. *Of course. I would be honoured.* She began to cry. They sat together holding hands while Tanner watched his children's program.

THE FUNERAL

Fatima's family organized the funeral and all the arrangements. The service was held at their Temple. Stella and Maria did not attend. They stayed at the house in High Park and looked after Tanner. William assured them that this was the most useful thing they could do for him. He didn't want Tanner traumatized by all the grieving friends and family.

Tanner seemed subdued and was missing his mommy. He didn't seem to understand where she'd gone and would ask for her from time to time. Stella took the rest of the week off work. She read him stories, and played with him, and hugged him when he was within hugging reach. Maria did the same. He was an affectionate little boy and didn't seem to mind all the extra attention foisted upon him.

Maria insisted that they try to keep him in some sort of a routine. She planned a schedule that included healthy snacks, fresh air, play time, and two short naps each day. Stella was amused by her grandmother's approach and thought she'd have made a great primary teacher. *It wasn't for nothing that I became a teacher myself,* she thought.

William had taken to sleeping in the guest room with Tanner. He didn't seem to want to go home in the evening. Stella was sleeping upstairs, in the old flat that had once been her father's. Maria was kept busy planning meals and making sure everyone was organized.

One night, when Maria and Tanner were asleep, Stella stayed up late to talk to her father. *Grandma is really happy with all of us staying here. I think she's enjoying the company.*

I know, agreed William. *She's in her element.*

I'm worried she'll be lonely next week when I go back to work.

Yes. I think she will be. She's been terrific.

I wish there was something I could do. I don't want her to be lonely.

Well, we're going to have to get on with our lives. I have to get back to work too.

What are you going to do with Tanner while you're at work?

I'll have to hire a nanny or a housekeeper of sorts. I've already called an agency.

But it will be a stranger. Someone you don't know.

I don't have a choice. I have to get back to work.

What if she's not nice to Tanner?

Stella, I don't know. I'm just trying to figure it all out.

I have an idea.

What?

Why not ask Grandma if she'll come and supervise at your house for a while? You know, during the transition.

William was thoughtful. *I'm not sure she'd want to leave this house. She likes her routines. But it would be helpful. And really nice for Tanner. He loves her.*

You could ask her in the morning. See what she says.

I wouldn't want to pressure her.

I don't think she'd feel pressured. I think she might be pleased to help.

Your mother might not like it.

I don't think Mom will care, Dad. She's a lot busier now. She goes swimming every morning, and she said something about a trip to California with her new friend. I don't know if they're serious about going, but she's in a really good mood these days.

So, are you sure I should ask her?

Ask who? Mom or Grandma?

Your grandmother.

Yes. See what she says. Even if she comes for a week that would help, wouldn't it?

MARIA'S RESPONSE

Stella busied herself in the kitchen the next morning while William talked to Sophia in the living room. When she finally joined them, it was pretty clear that Maria was thrilled to be asked. William was offering to buy her a suitcase.

I don't need so much things, William. A couple of dresses. Some shoes. No reason to waste money.

Stella beamed at both of them. *So, it's decided?*

Yes, your grandmother has agreed to come help me out for a couple of weeks. Until we hire a nanny and get everyone settled into a new routine.

And I will do the cooking, added Maria.

You don't have to do that. I can pick up prepared meals from the grocery store.

Frozen food is no good. The vitamins get killed. It's not good for Tanner to eat frozen food. What else am I going to do all day long? I will do the cooking. Maria clapped her hands together and nodded at William. *And Stella will help me get ready,* she announced.

FAMILY

*D*o *you know that my ex-husband actually asked my mother to stay with him? Can you believe that?*

Didn't his wife just die?

Yes, of cancer.

And don't they have a little kid?

Yes, a boy.

And doesn't he have to work?

Yes.

Then it makes sense to me.

But she's not his mother!

Pam and Tony were heading across the parking lot towards the sports complex. Tony had driven them there. Pam was power-walking to keep up with him and feeling a little breathless. Tony, meanwhile, was sprinting along effortlessly. He stopped and turned to look at her. *Pam, this is a good thing. Your mother is lonely. Her husband just died. How long were they married, sixty years? William's life just got turned upside down. His wife died and he's grieving and he has to go back to work and he's got a kid to look after. It makes sense to me.*

But she's not his mother!

So? Who cares? We don't own people, Pam. We can't collect them like stamps or goddamn Royal Doultons.

You don't get what I'm saying. Pam was indignant. She wanted him to take her side. To support her in this. She was feeling seriously annoyed.

Oh, I get it all right. I just don't agree with it. Give the guy a break.

You're siding with him because he's a man.

Tony tilted his head and studied her. Then he began to walk in small steps around her. He was grinning.

What are you doing?

Walking circles around you, girl. Like the whole world is supposed to revolve around you. That's what you want, right?

Stop it! You're embarrassing me.

Good. You should be goddamn embarrassed. You're one holy pain in the ass.

Pam walked away from him, sniffing indignantly. *Did it ever occur to you that this might be hurtful? That my feelings might be hurt?*

Tony caught up with her easily. *Pam, I get what you mean, but it's crazy talk. Family is more than who you're related to, it's who stands by you when you need them. Through good times and bad shit. And families are messy. They're complicated.*

Pam nodded at him, agreeing reluctantly. *All I'm saying is, it would have been nice to be asked.*

CLINGING TO LIFE

Maria was packed and ready to leave the house. William had put her bags in the car and she'd emptied the fridge. *I would like to go to the park first*, she said. *Can we stop there on the way?*

William took Tanner to look at the ducks while Maria made her way to the benches. She sat down heavily. William glanced back and saw that, in her pink flowered dress, she made a vivid splash of colour against the grass.

Maria gazed out from her bench. She and Stanislaw had often sat on this bench together, in all kinds of weather and at every time of year. Stanislaw loved the park. It was an important place for them and she felt close to him here. *William and Stella are coming together in sorrow,* she told Stanislaw. *And soon Stella will be moving out on her own. Even Pamela is happy. I am going to help look after Tanner. Stanislaw, your family is good. We are looking after each other and everything is good.* A gentle breeze blew up from the pond. Sophia knew what it meant. Stanislaw was saying that he was happy to know this, happy to know that in their sadness they were clinging to each other, and clinging to life.

THE GREEN KERMAN

In the days and weeks after Fatima's funeral, Stella remained absorbed in worry for her father, for her grandmother, for Tanner. Still, it was a busy time. She and Tara went through the furniture in the basement and then spent their evenings ferrying it to the townhouse. Room by room, they set up their domain.

William had hired a nanny, a young woman attending university part-time. He'd also hired a part-time housekeeper, an older woman from Russia to whom Maria had taken an instant dislike. After only a few days, William let the housekeeper go. Maria had been unwilling to relinquish control of the kitchen, the laundry, and anything to do with Tanner. *There's no use trying to reason with her,* he told Stella.

Stella felt terrible for her father having to wrestle with such problems in the midst of his grief. She got up early Saturday and arrived at William's house just as he, Maria, and Tanner were sitting down to breakfast. Maria had made blueberry pancakes. Stella heaped up a plate and joined them at the table.

We have something to discuss, said her father.

Yes, said Maria. *Something to discuss.*

Your grandmother and I are talking about renting out the house on Indian Grove for a year. She'd like to stay here with us and help me with Tanner. Next year he'll be ready for full-day kindergarten, and then we can reassess the situation. In the meantime, Maria has offered to stay.

Oh! That's great! Stella looked at William and then at Maria. *I think that's fantastic.*

William hesitated. *We wondered how your mother would feel about it.*

That's a tough one. Stella paused. *To be honest, I don't think she'll like it at all. But why should that really matter?*

Maria looked worried. *She might say she can't see me here.*

I can pick you up, Grandma, and you can visit at my place. I want you to see it anyway. We're moving in tomorrow. Sunday will be our first night there.

Well. It's settled then, said William. *We have a plan.* He sat back in his chair.

Besides, said Stella, *she's going on that trip to California with Mr. Dinapoli.*

Tony Dinapoli?

Yeah. Do you know him, Gran?

Know him? I saw him grow up. He was crazy, always jumping and bouncing. His parents lived in the neighbourhood. What is she doing with him?

They're new old friends. They've been swimming together almost every day at the sports complex. She seems to be a lot happier.

Tony Dinapoli, hmmph.

William was silent as Stella and Maria talked. He was pensive, and full of wondering. *Stella, I'd like you to help me with something.*

Sure, Dad. No problem.

She followed her father to the upper landing, where a ladder was leaning against the wall in front of the Kerman carpet. *I need you to help me take this down.*

What are you doing with it?

Just a minute and I'll tell you. William climbed the ladder and unfastened the wooden dowel from the brackets. He passed the carpet down to Stella, asked her to slip the dowel out, and then returned the dowel to its place. The wall looked empty, like a frame without its picture. William climbed back down.

It looks naked, Dad. Are we putting something else up?

No, I don't think so. I need to leave it like that for a while. To remember the way it was. William stood back from the blank green wall and looked at it sadly. He put his hands in his pockets and tried to choke back his emotions.

What are you going to do with this? Stella stroked the Kerman as she spoke. *It's so special. I hope you're not going to hang it in the basement or something.*

No, I'm not. It's a gift, Stella. From Fatima. She wanted you to have it for your new house. William laid one hand on her shoulder and the other on the rug. *She made me promise that I'd give it to you and that you'd know it was from her.*

Oh my God, I can't accept this. Stella put it carefully back in his arms. *It's too valuable.*

It is very valuable, but not just because of its price. This rug came with her family when they immigrated. It belonged to her great grandparents on her mother's side. It's been in her family for a long time. And it may not even have been new when they got it. The green is from insect dye.

Stella nodded. *Yes, I remember Fatima telling me that.*

She wanted you to have it. William held out the carpet and Stella took it from him.

Every carpet contains a meaning or a blessing. The green in this one is meant to soothe, to offer renewal and a sense of harmony. This was Fatima's wish for you.

Stella hugged the carpet and smiled at her father through her tears. *It's beautiful.*

William's face was marked by sorrow, but he smiled back.

ACKNOWLEDGMENTS

Although this is a work of fiction, I referenced some significant moments in history. Both of my parents lived through the devastation that took place across Europe during WWII. My understanding of the history of the period began with their stories. I am also indebted to several published accounts of trauma suffered by women in Iran during the Revolution. I apologize for any inadvertent inaccuracies, omissions, or misrepresentations I may have committed in the text.

My thanks to Chris Needham and the supportive team at Now Or Never Publishing. Thanks also to Donna Morrissey who provided challenging critiques on early drafts of the manuscript. Karen Alliston polished the final draft for me with her usual perceptiveness and skill. Angie Littlefield, my long-time mentor and friend, has always encouraged me and believed in the importance of this story. So many other people have enriched my writing life with their interest, care and support that I dare not attempt naming them all, lest I inadvertently forget someone. They know who they are and I thank them. And finally, thanks as always to the two men closest to my heart, Michael and Andrew Black.

The Carpets

For those interested in the carpets described in the book, the following may provide a helpful reference:

Black, David, Editor, *The Macmillan Atlas of Rugs & Carpets: A comprehensive guide for the buyer and collector* (New York, Macmillan Publishing Company, 1985).

Black, David and Clive Loveless, Editors, *Woven Gardens: Nomad and Village Rugs of the Fars Province of Southern Persia* (London: David Black Oriental Carpets, 1979).

Bosly, Caroline, *Rugs to Riches: An Insider's Guide to Oriental Rugs* (New York: Pantheon Books, 1980).

Eiland, Murray L. and Murray Eiland III, *Oriental Carpets: A Complete Guide* (London: Laurence King Publishing, 1998).

Purdon, Nicholas, *Carpet and Textile Patterns* (London: Laurence King Publishing, 1996).

Schlosser, Ignaz, *The Book of Rugs Oriental and European* (New York: Bonanza Books, 1963).

Valcarenghi, Dario, *Kilim History and Symbols* (Milan: Electa, 1994).